12

Valid For All Countries

stories by

Desmond O'Grady

University of Queensland Press

By the Same Author
A LONG WAY FROM HOME
EAT FROM GOD'S HAND
DESCHOOLING KEVIN CAREW

Published by University of Queensland Press
St. Lucia, Queensland, 1979

Typeset by Press Etching Pty Ltd, Brisbane
Printed and bound by Silex Enterprise & Co., Hong Kong

Distributed in the United Kingdom, Europe, the Middle East,
Africa, and the Caribbean by Prentice-Hall International,
International Book Distributors Ltd, 66 Wood Lane End,
Hemel Hempstead, Herts., England

Published with the assistance of the Literature Board of
the Australia Council

*National Library of Australia
Cataloguing-in-Publication data*

O'Grady, Desmond, 1929-
    Valid for all countries.

    ISBN 0 7022 1368 3
    ISBN 0 7022 1369 1 Paperback

    I. Title.

A823'.3

For Edward and Winifred

Contents

Acknowledgments

Acknowledgment is made to the publications in which these stories have appeared: *London Magazine, National Times, Bulletin, Quadrant, Southerly, Solidarity* (Manila), *Westerly, Sun* (Melbourne). Since first publication, some stories have been revised and some titles changed.

Sterner's Double Vision

WHEN THE RAIN, which had been hammering the galvanized iron roof, stopped as abruptly as it had started, Henry Sterner found a new irritant in the voice which carried from a nearby table. Less for its depressing cadence than for what the sharp-faced fellow, in white shorts and shirt, said about Papua New Guinea's imminent independence. The speaker told a fellow drinker that, with guidance from the whites, the locals should be able to run the country although services would deteriorate.

Sterner heard it as patronizing but was surprised that it set his bile flowing. He put it down to heat exhaustion. A brown man's country. He would be glad to board the plane to return to the States.

When he fell into conversation with the speaker, after a waiter had confused their orders, it satisfied Sterner to discover he was Father Lowry, parish priest of Baroka. The smug mentality, Sterner told himself, was a giveaway. Sterner explained he was an anthropologist investigating tribesmen's attitudes to sacraments.

Lowry's lean features lurched with surprise at such brashness. An amateur confronted by a professional, thought Sterner, lighting a cigar.

"They'll tell you only what you want to hear," warned Lowry, "you've got to get to know them before they'll reveal their real feelings."

1

"It's a question surely," said Sterner, scowling at the strong beer, "of how you go about it."

Sterner was an earnest conversationalist who took things to heart but he could not continue: his chair was pushed aside by a impetuous flood whooshing towards the front of the Bird of Paradise hotel.

Lowry, laughing like a schoolboy who has staged a practical joke, explained that this sometimes happened after heavy rain. The drains on the hill backing the hotel were unreliable. Sterner, sour-faced, wrung out his trouser cuffs, squelched water from his shoes, dreading the surprises which could be in store for him in coming weeks. A charming place. For a second, he had thought that, by mistake, they had been subjected to the hosing down of the natives' bar at the end of each drinking and vomiting session.

Sterner hated field trips. He suffered in the tropics because his skin was pale as a turnip: even in Baroka, at 5,000 feet, his tender flesh sizzled in the sun. His scalp, beneath thin, sandy hair, burnt scarlet. Sterner had a white, floppy hat and used white zinc creams liberally, thinking of them, however, as napalm jelly.

Because he disliked field trips, things tended to go wrong. In the Sudan he had damaged an investigation by giving a Monroe university sweat shirt to a woman the Anuak considered a witch. In Ruanda Burundi, he had unwittingly offended a Watusi leader who subsequently created difficulties for the research team. Since then, he had not put a foot wrong but he needed to turn up something original to obtain tenure now that Monroe university enrolments were declining. Aggressive young men were bringing eye-opening reports from the field which made his painstaking articles outdated.

He drove himself hard in his investigation. He was working in conjunction with others making similar enquiries in Africa. Each day, with his hired pickup truck, he visited a different village. It was hilly terrain and Sterner found he was shortwinded and sweaty after the least exertion. He did not sweat as profusely as on the coase but still acidly.

When not interviewing, Sterner was at a loss. As a high-burner, he needed to be intellectually refuelled with regularity. There was little stimulus in Baroka, a small town strung between the wartime airstrip and the new airfield. At night it offered a choice between a pizza lounge and a cinema which advertised a variety of films but, since his arrival, had shown continuously *Travels with My Aunt.*

Of course there was always Father Lowry who was more than ready to chat when Sterner did not manage to avoid him in the street. Lowry was trying to wean the American from his air of monastic zeal about an unpleasant task. On the slightest of pretexts, he had told Sterner why he had spent fifteen years in Baroka. A missionary order's vocations director had visited the Star of the Sea convent he attended in Melbourne but, unlike several friends, Lowry had not left the classroom afterwards for a confidential chat. Sister Murtagh, pointing at young Lowry, had announced: "Your place is out there."

"I've got her to thank," Lowry had summed up with a deprecating smile as a local youngster wearing a "I gotta be free to be me" sweatshirt padded past.

Why does he have to tell *me*, asked Sterner who had not mentioned that he had been a Jesuit. Sterner wondered how he himself would have put up with such a posting. He was not cut out to be a missionary but at least the Jesuits gave a man proper training. If you spoke to Lowry about the distinctively Jewish Old Testament interpretation, Midrash, Sterner imagined, he would probably advise you to use more talcum.

Most nights Sterner sprawled on his loosely sprung bed reading. One evening he was enjoying a scholarly article, as it sparked biting phrases for his eventual reply, when a flying beetle butted him. The heavy black insect blundered against the bed lamp, then flopped on its back on the bedside table, vainly waving its legs. Sterner was surprised that such a barrel-shaped bug could fly at all. It stood for the excess he hated about the tropics, the virulent growth of flora and fauna as if the life force knew no limits.

He studied its feeble topsy-turvy paddling as if he had an enemy within his power. Then he took the day's *Post-Courier,* slid it under the insect and flung them both into the night. A horse had stood outside the hotel that evening incongruously munching a pineapple. The unexpected fermented beyond his window. But when he had asked Thompson, the hotel manager, if there were any dangerous animals in the district, the reply was "Only the Highlanders".

One Saturday afternoon, Sterner spoke to a group of natives who crossed the Baroka football ground carrying the gear for a sing-sing, a dance feast: larger-than-life bark paper models of pigs and birds, mud masks, and tapa-cloth drapes. They told him the sing-sing would take place at Timbark, in nearby Chimbu territory, the following afternoon.

Sterner, at a loose end, sought them. But at Timbark he was told the sing-sing had already been held. His grasp of pidgin, despite a cram course in preparation for his trip, was less firm than he realized.

Disappointed, Sterner strolled through the Timbark school grounds looking at the replicas of dwellings used in various New Guinea regions. Puffed, he paused in front of a Sepik river spirit house. The scowling face it turned to the world was his own occasionally glimpsed in mirrors. But sagging Sterner was a lie; the real, slim Henry Sterner, he reassured himself, was merely concealed by spreading flesh. Although it seemed a pair of hams hung from his cheeks, he told himself it was not too late to get fit on return to campus. Once in shape, he would grow a trim beard to enhance his appearance: it might transform the avian to the saturnine. He made his way to his pickup truck charged with new energy.

He must have taken a wrong turning on the way back to Baroka for, after forty minutes, the road became little more than a track which, contoured around a hill, began to climb and narrow. Sterner could not recognize a landmark in the hilly but open grasslands. The story of my life, he thought wryly, wishing he had stayed at the hotel to write-up notes, the landscape is laid out as clear as a map but still I'm lost. His petrol gauge winked red. The nape of his neck tingled with anxiety.

Intent on the broken track, he saw the native

with only the corner of his eye. As he eased his trouser's chafing crotch, Sterner realized how vulnerable he was to an arrow. Thompson's words came to mind: "Even if you knock down a pig, don't stop to apologize. They'll just as likely kill you — head for the nearest police station." If you knew where it was.

The native, who had neither bow and arrow nor grass knife, was looking at Sterner with curiosity rather than hostility. He raised a magisterial hand. Sterner slowed almost to a crawl although fearing it might be a fatal mistake.

A red Qantas airline bag hung from the native's shoulder. His face was long, lined, intelligent. A sprig of eucalyptus was attached to his navy blue beret. He wore a fawn sweater against his skin, khaki shorts and thongs. Almost hidden in the bush, Sterner now saw, were a short woman and a young boy.

"Master, no good you behindim disfellow road."

Sterner confessed he was trying to reach Baroka. The native, saying that he lived near Baroka, gave a complicated explanation of the way to the main road. Sterner had to climb further to a small clearing for space to turn. When he descended, he found the native, his wife and son waiting meekly as if to wave him on his way.

Feeling magnanimous, Sterner stopped. The native, who said his name was Michael, explained that he had been to a sing-sing further up the hill. Sterner wondered if this was the sing-sing site he had sought. If he mounted in the pickup, Michael pointed out, he could indicate the route to Baroka. His smile was appealing despite the red which enamelled his teeth. Betel nut, Sterner surmised, or it might have been blood from the almost raw scrap of pork Michael held.

Encouraged by Michael, Sterner smiled for the first time since his arrival in Baroka and his incipient scowl disappeared as if it were merely a mask. Michael, his wife and son clambered into the truck's tray.

At the turnoff to the village, Michael said he hoped Sterner would be his friend and visit it. Maybe he only wanted a ride all the way home, Sterner realized, but he drove to the village. He would like to know a native outside the limits imposed by his survey. And a relationship with Michael would give the lie to Lowry.

There was a congregation of the curious, as in every village, for the arrival of Sterner's truck. Gumchewing, giggling girls, snottynosed, potbellied boys coated with dust. One of the excited group, a demure girl wearing only a loin cloth and neckband from which possum skins hung between her upright, succulent breasts, was Michael's daughter Christina. The crowd trailed Sterner through the village, the more daring touching him or his radio-recorder from behind. The village clearing was more extensive than any Sterner had visited. Coffee plants enclosed it on three sides.

Not only was Michael's hut bigger than most but it contained a table covered by a plastic cloth set with knives and forks. At the centre of the table, an empty tomato sauce bottle had pride of place. It struck Sterner as decidedly odd but he made complimentary remarks.

Michael led the way to a second hut where he

stabled his pigs. Chewing still on his shred of pork, emanating pride of ownership, he stood in the full path of the nauseous odour which issued from the hut. His wife, who kept a respectful distance, radiated pride in her husband. Their son dived through the low door to shout at the pigs. Sterner was overpowered by heat and stench.

A mottled grey pig, oinking, waddled around the side of the hut which many native families would have been happy to inhabit. Michael dived on the pig, a heaving mass of sensibility attentive to its master. With a finger he explored the animal's rear. "Him he got sick," he told Sterner after his display of veterinary skill, "me no savvy what name medicine belong straightim disfellow sick."

Such a self-satisfied man of property, Sterner decided, would welcome an interview. Switching on his recorder, he questioned Michael about his possessions. Michael replied readily. I can lead from this to his background and beliefs, Sterner told himself, an in-depth study more valuable than the survey.

When he did not have to travel too far on his survey, Sterner visited Michael's village in the afternoon. His excitement survived even the trial of Michael's calm insistence on genealogical detail which rivalled that of the Old Testament. It took Madame Dieterlein seven years to get on terms with the Dogon, Sterner recalled, but look where he was after only seven weeks. So much for negative Lowry. Sterner foresaw that even the academic Mafia, which he felt was ganging up against him, would be impressed by the results.

Sterner did not breathe a word of his activity to

Lowry. When they happened to meet in Baroka, Lowry would ask about the survey but he was more interested, Sterner found, in holding forth on the natives. Sterner considered Lowry's views bigotry masquerading as shrewdness but, consoled by his secret project, he humored the priest. The first he will know what's going on, Sterner promised himself, will be when I send him my monograph on Michael.

Sterner began to find presents left at the hotel when delays on his survey trips prevented him visiting Michael of an afternoon.

First, fruit: papaya, pawpaws and banana-passionfruits. He found it a touching gesture.

Next, a cute piglet. He had a hellish night with the animal squealing and squeaking whether he kept it in the room or tried to leave it in the corridor. When it finally slept, he dreamt of slaughtering swine but, on waking, its baby-soft flesh gave him pause. It squealed all the way home in the truck.

A few days later, Christina. As when he had first seen her, she wore only a loin cloth and possum skins but, for the occasion, she had henna'ed her hair. Christina placid, Sterner abashed. He imagined, accurately, that everyone in the foyer was watching him. What would Thompson think? The comments in the bar . . .

Barely aware of what he was doing, Sterner took her to his room. She sat on the edge of his narrow bed, one hand in another, her trustful eyes on him. Her breathing was as light as that of a serene sleeper.

Women provoked Sterner to pyrotechnical displays of erudition but such an evasion was impossible with Christina. Never good at small talk, he had to invent patter in pidgin. Christina replied sweetly, becoming animated only when she spoke of her father's new piglets.

The conversation was banal but Sterner's emotions were complex. Perhaps, unlike other women, she would not say anything about body odour or bad breath. He was tempted to take possession there in his alien room but fear of the uncharted prevailed. He dared not wait for the following day as he had with the piglet but returned her that evening. She enjoyed the ride.

Just as well he had to be home for first classes within days, Sterner concluded, for Michael's attachment was becoming an embarrassment. Sterner mentioned he was about to leave before he mounted his truck after a long, last recording session.

As he avoided potholes on the descent from the village, Sterner puzzled over Michael's reaction. It was as if he had suffered an internal landslide which doused all lights. You would say the soul went out of him, Sterner mused, if you used such anachronisms.

The following afternoon, he conceded himself a respite. Although he dreaded being taken as a tourist, he went with other hotel guests to a gumi race. Gumis are inner tubes of airplane tyres which natives race down the rapid local streams. Thank X, Sterner reflected, that he was unlike the suckers who paid good dollars to fly to New Guinea for such pleasures.

On his return, his radio-recorder, with the complete set of Michael tapes stored in it, had disappeared from his locked room. He looked at the corner where the recorder had lain as if it had been spirited away that instant. Ripped apart by the loss, weakened by the heat, he felt at the mercy of thieving savages. He knew Michael was the culprit. An immediate visit could surprise him into admitting his exploit: after all, for weeks he had been treating Sterner as his father-confessor.

Only the youngest children gathered at the arrival of Sterner's familiar truck. As Sterner approached, Michael, his tank-commander beret tipped jauntily, clambered from a cooking pit beside his hut.

"Good-day master. You go back long place belong you?"

Although Michael still addressed Sterner as master, he no longer smiled. Obviously their relationship had altered but Michael, far from being embarrassed, presented an impenetrable facade. Michael's black eyes, large and liquid, studied Sterner who, as never before, felt the man's colour opposed to his.

"Michael me like say 'thank you' long you. Time me come up long place belong me, me like writim big fellow talk belong you," Sterner found himself wheezing as if he had run uphill from Baroka. Simply saying that he intended to return home to write Michael's story was as exhausting as shifting heavy furniture. No wonder they could not think straight if continual detours were necessary to say something in pidgin.

"You stealim story belong me," said Michael, face as inexpressive as a coffee bean, with a level stare which suggested he did not distinguish between Sterner and other thieves, "another fellow he stealim long you, two fellow he one kind trouble belong me."

Sterner struggled to explain that, without the tapes, all his work was wasted. He felt drained for it was futile. Fattening pigs made sense but how could Michael understand a man's work as persuading others to talk into a recorder? The pig-sty stench reached Sterner. The recorder, he was sure, sat provocatively close in Michael's hut.

He told Michael that without the tapes he would not be able to eat. But how could he make Michael see a vast campus streaked with greying snow, a department where neat reports cooled the sounds recorders brought from tropical regions? The reports became weapons in iternecine tribal fights more vicious than anything natives knew, yet Michael was sending him into combat unarmed. Michael was unmoved by Sterner's forecast that he would go without kaikai. He knew whites always ate and Sterner, by the look of him, more than most.

And then Sterner shouted, as if he would batter comprehension through Michael's thick skull, "I have to have those tapes — they're my life." But it would be truer to say they were Michael's.

"You fellow life?" asked Michael. Was he dubious of the sound of "life"? Or of its appropriateness? He seemed to lean over Sterner.

"All the same pig belong you," Sterner slipped back into pidgin. "Suppose man no good he stealim all together pig belong you — all right you make him what name now?" Sterner, removing his white hat, dabbed his forehead.

Michael, chewing as usual, offered Sterner shelled

peanuts from his airline bag. Irritated by the casual gesture, Sterner waved them aside. He did not want anything from that dirty brown hand. By then, on second thoughts, he accepted the nuts in case the offer meant reconciliation.

"Me savvy long stink belong pig belong me," Michael said masterfully.

Sterner calculated the risks of rushing the hut grabbing his recorder and fleeing. Michael, although tall, was scrawny but some of the village men had given an exhibition of their arrow-firing ability. Brains rather than brute force must prevail; he would pretend to depart but return better prepared. It was a measure of his desperation that he sought Father Lowry. The priest's authority could give him access to Michael's house.

Sterner had sat through Mass before asking Lowry to accompany him. It confirmed the impression gained from his survey that the missions had trivialized the faith they brought and emasculated native beliefs. Natives who had known the awe of blood sacrifice had a tame surrogate in the eucharist. In turn, they reduced baptism to wash-wash, the Trinity to God three-one. To Sterner's superior eye, everything was at a lace and lilies level which must have been imported from Sister Murtagh's class at Star of the Sea convent.

The Old Testament reading recounted how Moses' people smote their enemies in battle as long as the leader's arms were held on high. There was rapt attention, the only noise a windswayed branch of a eucalyptus scraping a window, and Sterner imagined the tribesmen were taking tips on how to win their next clash. The intensity of their absorption, however, somehow unsettled him. Towards the front of the church were a few other whites but Sterner felt strongly what before had only been a fleeting intuition: that he was ethereal among these brown people, that they could look right through him. He linked it with a recurrent boyhood nightmare where he, dead and composed of a milk-weak white substance, was subjected to inhuman tasks until he awoke, terrorized, sweating.

At the end of Mass, the congregation sonorously sang "Star of the Sea" in pidgin. Trivializing the banal, Sterner thought impatiently, resisting the rhythms familiar from his boyhood. For him, the nadir of baby talk was reached with the pidginizing of "Mother of Christ watch over me" into "Mama belong Kraist lukluk long me". What could a protectress from marine misadventure mean to a mountain people who had never seen the sea?

Keeps his flock childish, Sterner concluded as the truck climbed, because his faith is preserved by a carapace of ignorance. Sterner would like to have told Lowry that the Dead Sea scrolls showed Jesus was an Essene, that his religion was what head-strong Paul had made of the Nazarene. He wanted to force Lowry to face the void but, as he needed the priest, refrained from challenging him. Lowry said that although he did not know the village, as it was Lutheran, he thought he could convince Michael to invite him to his house.

Michael, still solemn, did so. The table, with its plastic cover, knives, forks and tomato sauce bottle, stood unchanged as if it were a stage property. The recorder could not be seen nor was there anywhere such a bulky object could be hidden.

14

In the local dialect, Lowry talked lengthily with Michael about his pigs. Sterner was struck by the similarity between their lean, lined faces, their scrawny bodies. He regretted that he had matched clerical obtuseness against native cunning. The police, he realized, would have to be employed against Michael.

Lowry's purr of satisfaction was almost audible when they left.

"Suppose he denied everything," said Sterner as he weaved the truck among the potholes.

"Didn't even pop the question — unnecessary. Michael is a superior type. Thinks if he behaves like a dinkum Aussie, he'll get the cargo the white man enjoys."

Sterner did not want to be lectured by Lowry whose flat voice irritated more than ever. He wanted only his radio-recorder.

"Elementary, my dear Watson. Poke about in their cemetery — discreetly. Where the ground has been freshly broken, I'll bet you find your talktalk machine."

Sterner, nauseated by the absurdity, wondered if he could cut his losses by keeping his original plane booking. Had Lowry's brains been addled by too much "lukluk long me"?

"Did you ever ask yourself, Sterner, what you were doing for Michael?"

What was he supposed to do? Pay him? When the man had sought friendship? Sterner resented this catechism, he loathed Lowry treating him like a backward pupil.

"Didn't you ever ask why he was so cooperative?"

Lowry was leading the American into it slowly as if he were the academic equivalent of a camera-laden tourist.

"Took you for a ghost, that's why, a spirit, an ancestor."

Sterner kept his eye on the road but recalled that in church he had felt a photographic negative compared to the native congregation. It somehow confirmed Lowry's outlandish claim. He sensed Michael and Lowry were allied, that they had more in common with each other than he with either of them.

"It made sense of your questioning him so relentlessly." Lowry, damn his small mind, was enjoying himself. Sterner doubted if the priest would have the imagination to concoct such a story merely to discountenance him.

"Doesn't make sense to me."

"Doesn't have to. He explained his lineage because he was sure you were an ancestor returned as a white ghost. Obviously you'd come to check his ancestry before handing over the cargo his ancestors had made in heaven. Michael, by village standards, is a big man, but he wants to be bigger. When you had the full story, he thought you'd render justice, deliver the cargo."

Lowry paused as if he had a congregation on the edge of their pews. "Instead of that, all he got from you was a casual goodbye. He realized then you were a white impostor, pretending to be an ancestor in order to waylay his cargo for yourself. The white men do it all the time: look how prosperous they are."

Sterner was silent. It was the logic of the mad —

or of the deprived. He knew some natives practised rituals known as cargo cults through which they hoped to obtain the white man's goods. But he had believed they were confined to the north coast.

"What would you do after such a disappointment?"

Sterner pretended to concentrate on guiding the truck through a swarm of boys playing on the road. Lowry explained that the consequential thing was to plant the story box where the real spirits would heed it.

Hokum, thought Sterner, but after he had delivered the priest he asked himself what if he's right? It was his last chance. Under cover of dark, he would explore the cemetery.

He drove back before dawn, hating the country which, he was sure, would make him an oddball if he were trapped there.

Parking at a distance, he walked as quietly as possible to the cemetery, hoping any observers would take him as a ghost immune from arrows. He could have been guided by his nose. The cemetery, a cleared space with a few flowering shrubs as the only embellishment, provided an olfactory moral on corruption. The pervasive smell's origin was obscure as corpses were buried, even if shallowly. Crouching, although he could not have said why, Sterner worked his way around the broad clearing.

Guided by the beam of a slim torch, he felt not a ghost but a dark man bent on an obscure rite beyond the white man's ken. He exhausted himself in his search but there was no sign of his radio-recorder. He wondered if Lowry had played a stupid joke on him, a cruel jest to recount when visiting neighbouring mission stations. Still the schoolboy prankster.

Finally, light from the eastern sky enabled him to make out shapes some yards away. A tepid dawn. What am I doing here, he asked, as he caught his breath. In the half-light he could not believe that snowtipped 15,000 foot peaks stood on the noon horizon. Sweat misted his forehead. A village dog barked perfunctorily. The crones would soon begin an unexceptional day and he was a rediculous white man more crazed then they could ever be.

Then, as the light waxed, it touched a steel point pricking the ground like a fresh shoot.

Scarcely believing, but sure what it was, he pulled the steel and it lengthened. Michael had buried the machine with the aerial half raised.

The loamy soil was soft and warm. Sterner's small hands tore it away on all sides heedless of the hard sticks mixed with leaves. Swallowing great gulps of air as if he could not get enough, he paused only when a thorny stick caught in his watchband. His fingernails were clogged, his forearms filthy, his heart thumped like a tomtom. The tearing nails were torn. It did not matter as long as his precious machine was undamaged.

What an epilogue it would make to the Michael story. Dawn in the highland cemetery, recollected among the snowdrifts, in the department library, at countless cocktail parties. Sterner, a peerless raconteur, never knew he was such good value.

As its outline emerged, he saw the machine was intact. Sterner succeeds. However the tape in the reel was soil-caked. He extracted the others from the storage space, knocking their cores to detach soil. Sterner keeps a cool head, he complimented himself, even in the mindless tropics. But as he detached one viscous reel after another, he discovered the tapes were fretted, lacey as Lowry's vestments, as fragmentary as the Dead Sea scrolls but even more indecipherable. Insect life was as virulent underground as above, a brown man's country. Kneeling by his machine, he realised he was thickly spattered with the porridgy soil.

Oh mother, he wished he had the release of tears, lukluk long me. Why me, abandoned in this godforsaken land pullulating with spirits? He seized the fecund soil and squeezed it, cursing both Michael and Lowry. He plunged his pudgy fingers into the magma, begging the termites to shred them like his spirit. But they gave no satisfaction. Within seconds, the soil around his fingers set cold, lifeless as cement.

He did not call on Lowry but caught a plane immediately to Moresby via Lae to connect with his international flight. He dropped the priest a note from his university.

Sterner's survey results were routine but acceptable. In time, he overcame his desperation at losing the Michael material. In fact, it became an alibi, the fish-that-got-away as academic favours continued to go to younger men. However he kept his more acid comments on his colleagues to himself and found a niche in the department. He recalled frequently his novice master's refrain: Water finds its own level.

He made an attempt to lose weight but there was nothing to keep him at it. The real, slim Henry Sterner was hidden for good by soft flesh. But it was less a burden under a mild sun. The only thing that melted on the campus was snow. Sterner would have been tranquil if he had not acquired double vision to add to his sense of void. Every now and again, he saw himself through New Guinea eyes as a ghost who was not carrying cargo for anyone.

A Shot of Damascus

AS THE SHOUT had made Phelan's finger jump on the shutter, the resulting photograph would be askew. He swore at the busybody across the bridge and wound the key of his old camera as a preliminary to another shot of the minaret with its witch's hat spires.

The fellow who had shouted was still staring hostilely at him, but Phelan counted on the tacit protection of the occasional passers-by and the soldier on duty at the other end of the bridge. However, as he focused again, the squat fellow crossed toward him barking reproof. His bullish head was not quite level with Phelan's shoulder. His thinning hair reminded Phelan of a laurel wreath as its tufts pointed in all directions along the rim of a forehead which was sweaty, even though it was a mild, spring afternoon. Phelan wondered whether he could handle the fellow if it came to a fight: he feared the busybody might butt.

Phelan spoke English, French and Italian without getting through to his censor, who kept up his quickfire Arabic as if the force of it, together with his outsize expressions and gestures, would penetrate the foreigner's dull brain. The soldier and the passers-by were indifferent to the confrontation.

Phelan leant the small of his back against the

bridge's parapet, tucked his camera protectively under one arm, and waited for the excited citizen to simmer down. He was gesturing toward the minaret, and as Phelan followed the gesture he saw that military trucks were parked in the courtyard alongside it. Did the busybody, who was now inviting him to walk off the bridge, imagine that he was photographing a military installation? But, if this was the case, why should he be upset rather than the soldier at the far end of the bridge?

Abruptly the vigilante pulled a pistol from the pocket of his leather jacket and Phelan's air of patient superiority vanished. For all the interest the soldier and the passers-by showed, as Phelan quickly noted, the pistol might have been a cigarette, and he suspected that it was empty. But he feared, nevertheless, that a bullet might rend the scene's unreality and his tender flesh. His lower back was suddenly cold, his nonchalance dissolved and he obediently accompanied the gunman off the bridge.

Phelan did not want to die in Damascus. He was not even on duty: he had journalistic assignments in several Middle East countries but Syria was not one of them. He had merely taken the opportunity to stop over in Damascus as a tourist, which was why he had been photographing the witch's hat minarets.

As a journalist he rarely took photographs. He was scornful of people who spent their travels slicing the world into a little box. His camera reflected this attitude and an assumption that a humanist must be incompetent with the latest mechanical gadgets. It was a vintage Kodak Brownie with an expandable image box.

Phelan had no need of a camera except to take photographs of, and for, his two children, for he himself was a camera. It was not merely that he had an exact visual memory; journalism had aggravated his natural tendency to record everything as a detached observer.

Coming off the bridge, he folded the bellows back and snapped the camera shut, reassuring his suspicious guard at the same time with sign language. The Syrian had slipped the gun back in his pocket and, satisfied that the foreigner was cowed, walked alongside him exuding an irksome self-righteousness and an odor which was part heavy perfume, part sour sweat. Instead of entering the courtyard where the military trucks were parked, the pair took the tree-lined street which was a continuation of the bridge, with Phelan reflecting that, in other circumstances, he would have enjoyed the walk.

Since his arrival the previous day, Damascus had made an overwhelming impression on Phelan: he felt he had been hit by a blast from the furnace of revolution. The dynamism of the city was bracing. All the buses, driven with an abandon which was proof of faith in Allah, had radios blaring at a deafening pitch. Martial music and impassioned speeches, which were the radio's sole fare, swept though the city with the buses. At street corners, television sets on high stands showed military men, chests laden with decorations, delivering emphatic speeches. Bookstands overflowed with publications such as *Peking News*. A stiff wind scoured the sky of clouds and held the hosts of green-starred red, white and black flags taut.

At night, on the hills overlooking the city, a huge neon sign lit up whose Arabic was translated for Phelan as "Long Live the Socialist Revolution".

In the afternoon he had watched a procession celebrating the achievements of Socialism: sputniks and other spacecraft occupied the major floats. Background to the jammering propaganda was the intact ancient city, with crowded market and empty mosque, to which had been added what would pass as an attractive French provincial town.

Phelan had observed pairs of soldiers walking hand in hand; he had lingered in the mosque where one of John the Baptist's heads was kept; he had eaten unidentifiable but delicious food in a small restaurant; he had walked by the swift-flowing river lined with neat French-style, glass-fronted restaurants; he had come to the bridge, noted with delight the witch's hat spires and had decided he would return to photograph them for his children.

I could have drawn the minarets for them, he told himself, as he strode beside his captor. Phelan tried once more to establish communication in scraps of several languages, then, finding that the Syrian was deaf to them all, he told him, in the most conciliatory tone possible, that he was an interfering, officious prig, that he should stop trying to live up to Syrian stereotypes or be booked for overacting.

They had reached the outskirts of the city and the Syrian was explaining something in his staccato manner. Evidently he was telling the tall, sandy-haired foreigner that they had reached their destination, for they turned into an asphalted courtyard where groups of men stood chatting. Some of them greeted the captor as if he were a hunter returned with a good bag. Taking Phelan by the arm, he half-helped, half-pushed him through a doorway. Here, a phlegmatic official, who ignored all Phelan's attempts to talk to him, took down the captor's account of events, then dismissed him.

Phelan felt the better for that. Now all he wanted was someone to whom he could explain the whole ridiculous episode. He was passed to a surly, slow-moving official who understood Phelan's faltering French but was sceptical of his explanation that, even though his passport showed he was a journalist, he was in Damascus as a mere tourist.

When the official told Phelan that he would have to refer the case to his superior, it increased the journalist's annoyance and aroused his anxiety. He realized that it may have sounded a little odd that he should be merely sightseeing in Syria, but decided to stick to the truth as he lazily thought himself beyond suspicion. He was reminding himself that he was the one who should be demanding an explanation from the authorities when he was summoned upstairs to Captain Khahil's bare office. As soon as Khahil introduced himself Phelan forgot about being a ruffled tourist and summoned his journalistic awareness: the interview would be a tough one. Khahil's ramrod back held him only at medium height but he had cool authority and spoke an exquisite French which put Phelan at a disadvantage. He had an aura of calm as if he moved and had his being on an isolated pinnacle. His spotless uniform must have been tailored for his slim figure: it was a sheer blue linen and as elegant as his movements which seemed rehearsed to perfection.

His eyes, too, were blue and quizzical, and dominated an acute, ascetic face. He read through the report of the incident, sitting rigidly at his tidy desk with lips pursed, like a headmaster. He asked Phelan for the camera and, when he did not succeed in opening the ancient contraption, handed it back, inviting Phelan to give him the film. "I hope they are not of high artistic quality," Khahil said facetiously.

Phelan told himself that it was probably a security officer's idea of a pleasantry and decided to play it very cool. He wanted to avoid handing over the film for the good reason that it had some identifiably Israeli shots on it, of the Sea of Galilee and Nazareth, taken solely for the children, of course. He was thoroughly alive, at last, to the implausibility of his story from the Syrian official's viewpoint. Phelan had travelled with double passports, one for Israel and one for the Arab countries, but he did not fancy explaining to the suspicious Khahil how he had shots of Israel when the passport shown on entry to Syria indicated only that he had visited Arab countries.

Stalling for time, he asked whether it was forbidden to take photographs of mosques or of military establishments and was told it was forbidden to take photographs "of the city". He thought of touching a pathetic note by saying the photographs were for his children but Captain Khahil hardly seemed open to sentimental appeals. Phelan feared that any further delay in handing

26

over the film would count against him when, once it was developed, he was called to explain the Israeli shots.

Khahil wound an elastic band around the film and placed it in the tray beside him with the precision of a surgeon. Phelan's mind was racing now, but on a closed circuit: he was circumcised but, if it was discovered, how could he explain it was a common practice in Australia, that he was a Catholic of dependable Irish extraction and not a filthy Israeli spy who had entered Syria under false pretences? If only there were an Irish pastor in Damascus to put him through the hoops so that he could prove his orthodoxy. He still had the penny catechism off by heart. Who is God? Allah. He saw himself stripped before Syrian judges, condemned for his telltale sexual organ, crucified for a faith he did not even share.

Phelan knew he had to hide the collapse of his confidence by making a show of offended innocence. He protested about the overbearing fellow who had arrested him, asking what was his authority.

Steepling his small hands, Khahil explained that the fellow was only a private citizen who may have been carried away by his zeal, but added that he was a patriot. "In these days," he said, as if challenging Phelan to contradict him, "we are all patriots to guarantee the security of the nation; soon all the enemies of Syria will be hanged."

Captain Khahil was explaining that he looked forward to that day, for it would allow him to return to Aleppo, but Phelan was only half-listening, worried lest his face reflect his inner turmoil. He was thinking of the decorated tile from the Jerusalem Mosque of Omar which lay at the bottom of his travelling bag. He cursed his irresponsibility; if discovered, he would look foolish as well as reckless.

He had slipped the blue-patterned tile under his coat as soon as he arrived at the Mosque of Omar, picking it from the fragments scattered during repairs to the building's ceramic frieze. It was not for the children: he intended to add it to the other curious fragments, acquired in similar ways, which decorated the terrace of his Roman apartment. But more than his magpie instincts were involved: it had also been a silly sort of adventure, a muffled echo of Christians going in disguise on pilgramage to Mecca. An Arab urchin who had seen him was a potential threat, but Phelan had slipped him some baksheesh, visited the mosque, whose interior did not match its superb exterior, and succeeded in carrying the tile past the guards at the compound entrance.

Phelan had had a moment's fear when a brusque customs official at Damascus airport had gone through his travelling-bag, but the tile was not found, buried as it was in Phelan's soiled clothing. Phelan had his response ready if he were challenged about it: it was merely a stray tile which had taken his fancy.

He was less comfortable about it now, however: could he stick to that bland answer if they were shouting at him that it was a sacrilegious theft from one of Islam's holiest shrines where Modhammed had taken flight for heaven?

This very minute, Phelan told himself in silent

panic, all the greater for his earlier excessive nonchalance, Captain Khahil's men could well be routing through his things at the Letakia hotel, digging out the tile, his second airline ticket, which was further proof that he had been to Israel, and even his copy of Muriel Spark's novel *The Mandelbaum Gate* which they might regard as a manual for spies. Phelan warned himself that Captain Khahil probably considered him as a threat to the nation: in a madhouse, he reflected, the sane are counted crazy.

Khahil was giving a reasonable explanation of the reigning unreason: that extraordinatry measures were necessary in an emergency.

"It would be unfortunate if you got the wrong impression, Monsieur Phelan," he said gravely, implying that it would be only M. Phelan's fault if he did, "for even though you say you are here as a tourist you are, of course, a journalist."

And a circumcised one at that, Phelan added under his breath.

"You say you live in Rome," the captain continued in a way which may have been merely conversational but could also express doubts about all Phelan's affirmations.

Phelan said that he had a Roman wife.

The impeccable captain thawed. "Mediterranean people are the best," he said, throwing his arms wide, "Hitler was wrong in that. I don't think he was an historian of good academic standing." He wrinkled his nose.

Phelan had no difficulty in agreeing. Khahil, pointing out in his chisselled French that Mussolini had done more than Hitler to liberate the Middle

East from the French and English yoke, said he admired the Italians but for the fact that they had hanged Mussolini. He hurried on to say that Hitler, who he has seen delivering speeches when, as a student, he had visited Germany from Paris, also had great merits.

Phelan guessed correctly that the first one was his Jewish policy. He objected mildly that this had not endeared Hitler to the Western world, but Khahil, in the tone of a man stating a truism, answered that the West was hypocritical.

Hitler's other great merit, according to Khahil, was to ensure order and discipline. "Only when the Arabs regain order and discipline will they once again be a great people," he concluded, as if he were the first to make such a comment.

Phelan felt he must advance a reserve to hide his unease. He asked whether discipline could be attained if, as he had found, citizens were allowed to threaten innocent people.

Khahil enjoyed the objection. He smiled remotely at the benighted liberal in his power, went to a cabinet under the window and extracted a bottle of Pernod.

"You're right to worry about uncontrolled violence, Monsieur Phelan," he said, pouring out two measures of the pineapple yellow liquid, "but here it is a question of controlled violence. I appreciate your feelings toward that fellow. But he is made to feel that he is participating in the revolution. Don't worry: he is under control. Those who go beyond a certain limit are hanged — and everybody knows it."

Phelan wanted to known how many were hanged each month.

Captain Khahil was very much at his ease. He drew a pale blue handkerchief from his jacket sleeve and dabbed slowly at his temples and upper lip. There was a whiff of scent, but it was far more discreet than that worn by Phelan's captor.

"What sense would figures have?" he asked, and lingered over his Pernod as if waiting for Phelan's answer before continuing. "People here have always been hanged. The novelty is that now they're hanged only for clear reasons and only to form a disciplined people."

Phelan sat unconvinced, thinking of his circumcision, his fragment of the Mosque of Omar, and whether he would meet the fate of those who overstepped their limits, Khahil's penchant for talking about hanging seemed unhealthy. Phelan regarded his Pernod as the suave offering made by police chiefs in second-rate adventure fiction before throwing their victims into solitary cells.

"You're familiar with Sorel, no doubt, Monsieur Phelan," said Khahil. Phelan came to with a start and his mind flicked to the French film star Jean Sorel, but then, in a misty recess of memory, he identified the reference to the philosopher of violence . Phelan's French conversation was highly stylized, limited to a small vocabulary and fixed forms. He had been pleasantly surprised to find that Khahil, unlike many Frenchmen, did not make him conscious of its shortcomings. His cramped style was now a help in hiding his ignorance. He ventured the safe opinion that no one had really put Sorel's ideas into action, then led on to Mussolini and Malaparte's works. He was, he told himself, home and hosed. Khahil was still riding his hobby-horse and Phelan guessed that he was continuing the discussions he must have engaged in at Parisian sidewalk cafes as a student, nursing a Pernod, and advocating the overthrow of French colonialists in Syria.

Phelan was reassured. He understood Khahil's pitch: that they were both cultured men, conversing in the language of culture. If violence was the subject, it was nevertheless violence to be controlled by an élite capable of disciplining fellows such as the one who had tackled Phelan on the bridge. Phelan was diffident of élitist ideas but was in no doubt that he would rather be accepted by the élite than be flayed on the feet.

"Intelligence without passions remains abstract," Khahil was saying, and Phelan noticed how restless his hands had become, "but passions get nowhere without intelligence. It would be an enormous satisfaction for that fellow who tackled you on the bridge if I threw you into prison. But when he finishes his duty, ours begins. He cannot understand that, he cannot see the revolution as a whole. His kind are bricks in a building which will be completed only in the future. A study of history, Monsieur Phelan, makes you admit that you cannot make bricks without straw."

"I'm not really a student of history, Captain," said Phelan "but I do know we've given up making bricks with straw."

"The revolution cannot proceed without sacrifices, Monsieur Phelan," said Khahil rapidly. "A people can be galvanized by struggle and a

32

vision. But some cannot grasp the vision, some must fall in the struggle. There are others to replace them. People are expendable: it's something you don't like to admit in the coddled, bourgeois West. Is there anything else?"

Khahil had become more emphatic and a little flustered. But apparently the re-education session was over, for as he concluded he rose, restored Phelan's passport and emptied camera and accompanied him to the door.

Phelan restrained himself from breaking into a run as he descended the stairs. Street lights were on, but he saw with surprise that the fellow who had captured him was still standing by the exit. Hands tucked into the pockets of his leather jacket, he stared morosely at Phelan, who would have liked to have chanced a flippant "salaam" but thought the better of it. He feared a bullet in the back, or, at least, a roughing-up, but he was allowed to walk off. He wandered through the city streets, as he did not want to ask anyone for directions, until he found his airline office and advanced his booking to the first flight available, which was the following morning, even though it meant going to Istanbul rather than Beirut as he had intended. He bought the local French-language paper to while away the night, then headed for his hotel.

He was tense with the thought that his room had been ransacked, but he found nothing out of place. The Mosque of Omar tile sill nestled at the bottom of his bag. After searching for a hiding place, he slipped it under the paper lining of the wardrobe. He would claim an earlier traveller must have left it there, if they developed his film with its shots of

Israel and came for him. That was his nagging fear. Khahil might have plotted all along to take him during the night, or, even if he were not so diabolical, he might want to put him through a real interrogation once the film was developed.

Phelan tested the lock on the door several times. It was not even normally firm but, in any case, it would have been no protection. He did not put on his pyjamas for the half-admitted reason that they would enable his circumcision to be seen more easily. He read the thin French-language daily a few times, tried to placate his anxiety-hunger with a bar of chocolate, then stood at the window watching the dominant neon sign on the hillside opposite and wondering whether it should be translated "Long Live the Socialist Revolution" or "Long Live Revolutionary Socialism". He tried to convince himself it was a distinction with a difference. Until now he had considered himself mildly leftist.

He attempted ineffectually to rest on the bed with his eyes closed, then opened *The Mandelbaum Gate,* which he had finished on the trip. After a few minutes he threw it aside for, although he admired it, in these circumstances its agile artifice irritated him. He stood at the window watching the neon hymn to revolutionary socialism fade like a bad dream with the advance of dawn. It was the last thing he remembered before he was awoken by stormtroopers banging at the door. The lock and key were dancing. Phelan sat up in his unspoiled bed in confused terror at the Arabic shouting. His head throbbed and he saw before him the implacable Khahil. Then the shouting, which was also in execrable French, began to unscramble.

"Hurry: car late for airport. Monsieur overslept? Monsieur sick?"

"I'm dressed and packed", answered Phelan. "Won't keep you waiting a jiffy."

He was deliriously happy in the car, which called at a house to pick up two of the plane crew. They invited Phelan in and, although he usualy avoided it, he drank with pleasure the concentrated black coffee they offered.

"Do you like this regime?" he asked provocatively. "It could be worse," one pilot answered sardonically " ... I think."

Phelan had to restrain himself from singing as the car made toward the airport. Daybreak seemed arrested as leaden clouds hung on the horizon. Frequently the car was forced off the road by cumbersome, dun green tanks which rolled in a long line toward the capital.

The last trap, Phelan mused, would be the airport: a soft-voiced official who would take him by the arm just as he was to submit to passport control and ask him to clear up a few details in a nearby cubicle. But he was convinced that he was out of the B-grade movie by now, that the fellow on the bridge was merely an excitable busybody and Captain Khahil a polite official who enjoyed reviving the theories of his schooldays. Phelan accused himself of an overheated imagination once he was involved and could not maintain a reportorial detachment. He regretted leaving the Mosque of Omar tile in the hotel wardrobe.

"And so we say farewell to Damascus, city of Oriental mystery and revolutionary socialism," he Fitzpatricked to himself as the Caravelle gained height, "where the setting sun of Sorel throws its dusky pink fingers on the crescent moon of Islam." The hostess passed with the morning papers. Phelan chose the only non-Arabic one, the French-language daily.

Captain Khahil was staring at him from the front page. He had been shot by a fanatic as he left his office last evening. Four bullets had hit him as he descended the steps. The killer, whose photograph did not appear, would be hanged today.

Phelan, exhausted, dozed on the flight to Istanbul, but woke several times to reread the item. He saw red on blue, Captain Khahil spurting blood to stain his spotless uniform. Even though the killer's photograph did not appear, Phelan was sure he knew the laurel-wreathed face of this poet of the revolution.

As he had to wait for a connection in Istanbul, Phelan decided to stay overnight and catch up on lost sleep. Despite the low ceiling of rain-laden clouds which made the Bosphorous grey, he enjoyed Istanbul. After Damascus, it was shabby, large and relaxed. The cars were mainly old, outsize American monsters; people fished from the wharves and cooked their gleaming catch on charcoal fires; there were ferry rides. He felt at home as in his Sydney. Wandering along the waterfront, he came to a statue of Ataturk, which reminded him that here, too, there had been a revolution forty years ago. But Istanbul, rather Constantinople, had survived. He resolved to return to Damascus and photograph the witch's hat minatets for his grandchildren in the first years of the third millenium.

Life, Debts and Miracles of F. X. Horgan

SHORTLY AFTER he had turned fifty, Father Francis Xavier Horgan began hearing the voices. Although he had been practising heroic asceticism, he suspected they were not angelic in origin for the first, which came during his end-of-Mass prayers for the conversion of Russia, was "Go Pretty Boy for the Welter."

Horgan shook his head, as if to dislodge a flea from his ear, and caught up with the congregation asking God to do something about the Bolsheviks. He knew that Pretty Boy, a sluggish starter, did not stand a dog's chance. Pretty Boy romped home at fifteens.

As he went about his duties in the following days, FX contemplated the fact that if he had punted $400 on Pretty Boy, he would have wiped out the parish debt. Must have been a tip from the best source, he concluded.

A short time before, he had become parish priest in one of Perth's outlying suburbs. He had resolved to justify the trust of the bishop who had accepted him after his addiction to racing had made him a blacksheep in Melbourne archdiocese.

Fellow curates in Melbourne had not appreciated Horgan's disappearance on Saturday afternoons when confession lines were longest. At times he would hear some confessions before going walkabout, other times he would not even front. Challenged, he pleaded claustrophobia in the confessional. This did not placate hard-pressed colleagues who could hardly advise impatient penitents to seek Horgan at Flemington, Caulfield or Moonee Valley racecourses where his friends plunged after hearing his lightning-quick calculations.

His own punting was neither heavy nor profitable. As his was a pure passion, this did not discourage him. His father, a successful businessman, had been a keen punter but even before he took young Francis Xavier to the racetracks, the boy knew all about the sport of kings from long hours spent over *The Sporting Globe.*

His passion continued unabated through his seminary years. As a young curate, he had plans to form a syndicate with lay friends to buy a racehorse. Nothing came of it but, on his free days, FX liked visiting stud farms just as he would happily attend midweek city meetings and country races without laying a bet.

But it was betting which finally cruelled his pitch in Melbourne. He was shunted from one parish to another until the archbishop told him he would have to hear confessions Saturday afternoons or else. Dammit, you have a Race Mass every year before the Cup, FX would like to have protested, but was abashed by the melancholy authority of the man who was archbishop at that time. FX spent his

Saturdays nailed to the confessional but began to bet heavily, and unsuccessfully, with backlane starting-price bookies. As the backlanes were thick with parishioners, word circulated.

The archdiocese had its share of boozy priests and womanisers but FX was a worse headache.

"Father Horgan seems to lack even normal foresight," said the archbishop in his pleasing brogue when told of FX's losses, "What sort of spiritual guide can he be?"

To tell the truth, Father Francis Xavier Horgan brought to mind a form guide more readily than a spiritual guide. Powerfully built, he had the face of a racetrack clocker. His cheeks were glazed as if winddried. His parched lips seemed stuck together: he did not open his mouth readily and apparently it hurt him to smile. His face was wooden, except for one eye whose drooping lid made it look shrewd, but he talked as intensely as an evangelical preacher, although FX's message usually concerned what was going in the handicap the following Saturday.

FX's dog collar sat uneasily on a neck which should have been open to the sun. His black clerical hat perched jauntily at the back of his head. He was serious enough about being a priest but on Saturday his heart beat in time with horses' hooves. He should have been chaplain at Flemington racecourse.

Only someone as trusting as the auxiliary of Perth, a crony since seminary days, would have given him another chance after Melbourne. The surprises of grace are infinite, the more venerable said, when they learned FX was a new man who spurned the temptations of the racetrack: that was his heroic asceticism. Take a swab, his former curates said when word of FX's new life reached Melbourne. The auxiliary of Perth died young but convinced that he had done at least one good deed. FX's parish priest soon followed in his wake. FX was a spiritual orphan with a flock of 3,000 and a parish debt of $6,000. It was then that he began to receive messages.

They were perfectly clear but rare, whereas the debt grew steadily. He was unsure whether to regard them as temptation or inspiration.

He knew Whitenose would win the Three-Year-Old Stakes as he was leaving St. Jude's, redolent with incense, following Benediction. After a struggle with himself, he decided not to plunge but confided in Clarrie Hickey who made a packet on the heavily built bay.

"Straight from the horse's mouth, I'd say, Frank," said Hickey, jumping out of his skin at the possibilities. "Don't worry I'll weigh in Sunday morning," which was a not-altogether convincing promise of a large contribution to Sunday's collection.

Hickey was a spruce, sharp little man who could have been a jockey. He ran a bakery but also shared FX's passion for horses. He owned one, Inkling, a fine-boned grey which had performed well on country tracks without being placed in the city.

Hickey frequently suggested that FX have a flutter. He redoubled his efforts after Whitenose's victory but, with a clenching of the will, FX stood firm. Each Saturday afternoon he was advising sinners that backsliding could only be avoided if they shunned occasions of sin. The first slip, he told them, was fatal.

His virtuous restraint, however, did nothing to diminish the parish debt which depressed him and his parishioners each time he mentioned it. He found himself thinking that his father, with his inventive business instinct, would have found an answer.

After a talk to the confirmation class at the local school, he knew that Soldiering On was the hope for the Derby but he did not pass word on Hickey. It was a lonely, pointless victory for him when Soldiering On came home at 7-2. At those prices, he would need to have invested heavily to cancel the debt. He regretted he had not punted on Whitenose.

FX now found the debt at the bottom of every cup of weak presbytery tea. He felt an old man as he walked the parish streets asking dully how he could shift its brute weight. The collections each Sunday were pathetic antidotes, the parishioners were clerks and working-class people at full stretch to clothe, feed and educate their children. FX wanted them to have a flash of excitement in their lives, he regretted harping on the debt.

As he led a class of twelve-year-old boys in the Stations of the Cross, he knew the remedy: Golgotha in the Maiden Plate. The meeting was at Kalgoorlie which confirmed his feeling that he had the inside running. As Kalgoorlie was over three hundred miles from Perth, he would be out of range of indiscreet eyes.

FX emptied the parish kitty. Golgotha's odds had lengthened to 25s by the time he plunged. It led all the way only to be pipped on the post. At the verdict, FX felt his heart stop pumping. Pins and needles stabbed his left arm. But he revived reluctantly, repeating Golgotha like an incantation. He had to borrow his train fare home from a strapper.

He confessed to Clarrie. "It was an each way tip," said Clarie, grinning craftily, probably piqued that FX had tried to make a killing on the quiet.

Alongside the snowballing parish debt, there was now another secret one. FX dreaded being caught with his hand in the kitty. Don't I get any credit for the temptations I withstood, he asked? Or had he been ignoring inspiration? "Never look a gift horse . . ." came to mind.

Clarrie advised him Inkling was a goer for the next country meeting. "I timed him to do two furlongs in 23 the other morning." Clarrie's eyes glistened greedily. Inkling did show signs, but he was a little too light-on to FX's expert eye.

He attended the meeting. Inkling flew home but finished a length from the third placegetter. FX was glad he had kept his hands in his pockets

He would wait for infused knowledge. He became assiduous, sitting back-breaking hours in the confessional, walking his shoes thin on home visits, preparing the parish school children for the sacraments. But illumination loitered. And the more zealous FX became, the more he feared exposure as a fraud.

Anxiety must have made him go along with Clarrie's suggestion. Clarrie supplied the money, FX flew to Melbourne to acquire from Australia's most eminent batterymaker his masterpiece. It was to make Inkling a sure winner at Kalgoorlie. The battery burnt in FX's palm as if it were a particle of hell. If it had been a packet of contraceptives, he would not have been more ashamed.

Unwittingly, the archbishop almost wrecked plans by asking FX to christen his nephew's child on the race day. The answer was hiring a plane which would reach Kalgoorlie in ample time for FX to install the battery. FX regretted having to put a swifty over the archbishop who, he imagined, would fall off his episcopal throne if he could see one of his parish priests being piloted to Kalgoorlie.

When his plane was within half an hour of Kalgoorlie, it was slashed by rain, cuffed by wind. The pilot, Atkinson, a small-featured young man who had taxied endlessly around the tarmac as if uncertain how to take off, said he would turn back to avoid a storm moving up from the Bight.

FX had placed sufficient money in Perth for Inkling's defeat to land him on a criminal charge. The advancing black clouds were his idea of the wrath of God.

His own wrath seemed capable of driving the plane straight through the boiling cloud-wall. Then the plane began bucking: when it dropped in an air pocket, FX cracked his head. FX's prayers for survival became more vehement than his orders to fly on.

Atkinson tried to skirt the storm. Although it hammered further north, the flight remained uncomfortably pneumatic until the engine cut. Throat dry, voice hoarse, FX sat silent as the plane glided to land beside a deserted football oval.

Faintly he asked if the engine could be fixed. He suspected there was nothing wrong with it, that Atkinson had landed because he was disgruntled. The pilot's face, chalky with fear, was surly.

Atkinson pottered with the engine as if it were his Saturday afternoon hobby. FX could see Inkling at the tail of the field, weighed down by the money he was carrying to the bookmakers.

FX climbed down, hating the aloof gums in the distance. The soggy ground reminded him that Inkling would be ill-at-ease on a wet track. FX felt the surge of straining horses, saw the iridescent flash of jockeys' silks. He was marooned. Even if he could have hitched a ride, it was too late to reach Kalgoorlie in time.

FX, hands in his pockets, chill wind putting a higher glaze on his cheeks, wondered if the traitorous plane could be a means of escape. But where? Come down halfway across the Nullarbor? He asked Atkinson how much juice was left.

"Just enough to get us back to Perth," Atkinson's forehead was corrugated. "Burnt it up on that buckin' joyride."

FX climbed back to his seat and slumped forward, feeling like a motherless child such a long way from home.

He saw himself as a boy pushing a bicycle, whose chain had broken, up an endless hill in Bourke Road, invoking Divine aid. He could not remember the outcome, only the intensity of his plea. Or again, while a seminarian, clambering over a rocky ledge, in the Grampians. Loose stones has shifted under his feet, rolling, then bouncing on their echoing way. He was afraid to go either backwards or forwards. An engine had begun thumping in the distance. It was some seconds before he realized it was his blood. Skin sentient with fear, he had flashed an SOS to Christ. But he had a direct line then.

What is the good of a God, he asked, if he doesn't help when most needed? Rescue me from this situation, he bargained, and I'll steer clear of race-course perdition in future. He saw the useless battery in his left hand as the germ of corruption, and closed his eyes to shut out the world.

Atkinson, still tinkering, invited him to turn on the plane's radio for the race. FX had not thought of that possibility. By the time it was tuned, Inkling and the other twelve competitors were taking their position in the starting stalls.

The race caller, whose measured rhythm would accelerate with the horses, described the favourite, Buckley's Chance, as well placed from the start. He ran through the field before he mentioned Inkling as hemmed in by the last bunch of horses.

FX crouched over the crackling set, his ruddy cheeks an intenser ruby, his shrewd eye vacant, as if hearing a life sentence. The caller had Buckley's Chance making light work of the heavy track but, as they came to the home turn, it faded while Andrea Doria and Inkling moved up strongly.

FX's hopes were ignited by the caller's excited litany. Inkling forced his way through on the inside as they settled for the run to the judges, sweeping past Buckley's Chance and with half a length on Andrea Doria. FX turned up the volume as the caller's hysteria peaked:

"But Black'nTan - is - coming - home - stoutly - on - the - outside -here - he - comes - look - at - him - go - making -up - ground - like - an - express - train."

FX could see him, huge, black as sin.

"Inkling's - fighting - on - gamely - in - the - run - to - the - post - Buckley's Chance - and Andrea Doria - dropping - back - through - a - bunched - field - Cracko'Dawn - moving - up - the - whip's - on - Blackn'Tan - got - his - head - in - front - on - the - line - but - I'll - leave - that - one - to - the - camera."

I've backed it all up, FX told Christ quietly but with his fists clenched. He was a big man. Come good now, he begged but would like to have threatened. Dried saliva lined the corner of his mouth. Just open the judge's eyes to Inklings' win, that's all — if You're really there. What's the good of stony silence when I'm tearing my guts out? Christ, come off Your highhorse.

Atkinson was asking if Horgan had backed Inkling each way but he had not heard. He concentrated on the caller's voice, now subdued: "Inkling it is: I thought Black 'n Tan had got up in the last stride but there's the judges' verdict after closely examining the print: Inkling, Black 'n Tan and Crack o' Dawn, which came from nowhere, third."

"Alleluia!" FX shouted, throwing his arms wide and remembering the battery crushed in his palm.

Palm Saturday, he thought, seeing his triumphal entry to Perth as a solvent parish priest.

His first impulse was to throw the battery away. His second was to give it to Clarrie but that would be to abet sharp practice. He decided to sell it back to its maker who, after all, otherwise would only make another.

All right, he told himself, when Atkinson finally took him aloft, so it wasn't a miracle just a great run by Inkling. But he'd honour his word all the same: Do a decent turn to Horgan and he'll return the compliment.

He was as good as his word, or better. He acquired a new buoyancy. He convinced people they could lick temptation. He reduced his contacts with Clarrie and kept away from racetracks. Only at the end of the year did he announce that the parish debt had been cancelled and he did not hint how. It was unprecedented. Throughout the archdiocese, his managerial ability and strong character were admired. It was rumoured that he ran five miles before breakfast each morning. He did not mind hearing all the confessions on Saturday afternoons.

When the city's biggest parish needed a new parish priest, FX was the natural choice. He was given a warm welcome and a fresh-faced assistant who was still looking for the answers in theological reviews. The parish debt, which had topped $130,000, seemed to have a life of its own. Insiders tipped FX as the next auxiliary bishop.

After many years on the outer, FX appreciated

the trust in him. He soon realized that a miracle was necessary to cancel the debt. However he battled against it with orthodox methods. He became irascible, grey, lined by worry. Smiling seemed to have become even more painful. He inaugurated a third collection at each Mass but it was like milking a dry cow. Frustrated by their lack of response, he would berate latecomers and those who loitered at the back of the church.

"Come on — there's room up front," he would thunder, "No good hiding behind the paper stand — or the baptismal font." Like driven sheep, they would edge forward looking for an early pew. "No need to be ashamed when you're about the service of the Lord," he would insist, getting a charge from such harangues.

He had settled for the long haul. Fellow parish priests now accepted him as one of their own, even if he was bad news for their whisky reserves.

The archbishop was always encouraging although, FX suspected, disappointed by his inability to dint the debt. One plunge, FX used to think when he reached the bottom of his Johnny Walker, could be sufficient to topple that debt. But he had turned his back on all that.

Besides, even though messages still came occasionally, he could not unscramble them. Maybe the signals were weaker. Or too much religious static blunted reception.

The Apostleship of Prayer intention for October was China. FX took it as a pointer to Fu Manchu in the three-mile event. Long March came from a long way back to win.

Something was coming through as he was leading

the rosary after evening devotions. A furtive additional sign of the cross scotched the distraction. He recalled it only when Simple Simon squeezed home in the weight-for-age.

He was ashamed when, at a crowded 11 o'clock Sunday Mass, what should have been "Dominus Vobiscum" involuntarily came out as "Dob it on Tony's cone." He remembered it when the weight-for-age the following Saturday was won by Ice-cream King.

Leafing through the *Australasian Catholic Record* in the presbytery after first Friday Mass, he knew that Herman Utix was the answer for him. But as he had never heard of it, he ignored the hint. Of course it was a winner, running away from Key Rigamorole with The Good News a poor third.

Psalm 22 leapt off the page as he was reading his breviary:

The Lord is my shepherd,
I shall not want;
He leads me by pastures green . . .

But Green Pastures was so short that an enormous outlay would have been needed to match the debt. Green Pastures won only on a protest. However, in the last race, a rank outsider, Lord Shepherd, came home. The doubles quote was 50 to 1, a gift to anyone who would trust his intuition. FX had to recognize the message had gone right past him.

His clerical hat was fixed squarely on his head, his dog collar no longer chafed. Horses for courses, he reminded himself, trusting he was on the right track. This life was losing its flavour which reassured him he was on a sure thing for the next.

Only when he heard a race broadcast did he doubt that he could stick it out to the finishing post.

But most Saturday afternoons, when the race-caller's muezzin cries riveted true believers, Father Francis Xavier Horgan was hiding in the confessional. A transistor as compact as a battery lay silent in his lap except in the rare pauses between penitents who appreciated his speed and his dry-lipped assertion that they could always make a new start.

Dip One Toe at a Time

Spectral, Martin Harkness told himself as he stood outside the Prague station noting the effect of feeble street lighting on decrepit buildings. *Dreary as well as eerie,* he added when he found that all Prague was in penumbra. That was when the psychologist he had met on the train drove him to his hotel. The psychologist, returning after an international congress, said he had ignored offers from the West as he did not want to leave his family and his Czech roots. He pointed out landmarks, explaining that the lighting was dimmed to save electricity. Martin's responses were designed to mask his bewilderment at the city's shabbiness.

The hotel, reputedly one of the city's best, completed the picture. The foyer's faded damask recalled an earlier period while the aged porter, wizened and obliging, was a contrast to the surly young reception clerks. Martin cautioned himself not to jump to conclusions. His intuition was quick but he rarely trusted it.

He had come to Prague after receiving a letter in Rome, where he taught high school English, from a certain Ignat Neruda. Neruda, a translator, sought eludication of points in one of Martin's short stories. It was the first time anyone had translated him, indeed he doubted that anyone read his stories. Otherwise, he might have continued writing.

Flattered, Martin had replied that he would discuss the translation when in Prague. Fanatical to go to Prague to discuss a few phrases, he realized. But after a Roman summer, he needed a change. Moreover, there was an implicit hope: that recognition would set him writing again, dissolving his conviction that nobody-was-listening, that everything-had-already-been said.

He had looked forward to Prague. Mildly leftist, he had visited only one other Communist country, Yugoslavia, enjoying its island-flanked coastline. All this made Prague's initial impact more disappointing. But the morning after arrival, he saw the city was anything but a dreary stageset. The seat of government, the hilltop castle with St Vitus' cathedral within its walls, was a proud silhouette against a pigeon-grey sky. The clocktower in the Old Town square tolled for Martin. Golden imperalism, dark spires and cosy baroque married.

The city was intact even if rundown. Communism is the only real conservatism nowadays, thought Martin, intrigued by the scarce traffic which crept at a hypnotically slow pace. Vintage cars were commonplace. Martin toyed with a film idea: a Czech couple escaping to the West in an old Skoda which they would sell for a fortune to a vintage-car buff. He could see someone debonair, Rex Harrison, say, in the part but his partner? Kin Novak? Wasn't she Czech? A madcap, harum-scarum vintage-car film and, he realized, quite unreal. He could not imagine the Czech couple. There was certainly a lack of glamour in the streets.

He had thought Prague would be rather like Vienna of *"The Third Man"*. And expected the

Mittel-European to be a Leopold Bloom figure, relishing the inner organs of beast and fowl, indicating his liver, heart and head when he wanted to signify courage, feeling or intelligence but getting them hopelessly confused.

That first sultry morning Martin typecast those he saw as opportunists who had made a party career, shifty informers or resourceful intellectuals, polyglottal, indestructible because everything was grist for reflection. The aged escaped categories: the old quarter's inhabitants, it occured to him, had seen all the permutations from the time Franz Josef was emperor. The quarter's name, Stare Mesto, intrigued him for in Italian it meant "to be mournful".

Drab clothes reduced the range of types. The great majority, he decided, were frugal housewives, penny-pinching clerks or tough factory workers. Some of the younger people, however, achieved style through long hair, blue jeans or miniskirts.

As Martin crossed a park on the way to Ignat Neruda's office, a man in grey slacks angrily shooed him off the grass. If Martin had known the language he would have objected but, gorge rising, he obeyed. The vigilante, accompanied by an equally squat and truculent woman, flashed a small plastic-covered identification card. "People's police", thought Martin, nostalgic for bourgeois repressors in identifiable uniforms.

When Martin reached the address, he discovered that the biscuit-brick building housed a publishing house and a writers' association as well as Neruda's literary quarterly. His arrival caused consternation. After traffic between one cubicle and another, a tall woman, who introduced herself as Karol Hvarec, explained that she had replaced the temporarily absent Neruda. She took Martin to a large room which, he guessed, would serve for editorial conferences and perhaps lectures. It made him think of a convent with its conversation parlours for guests who never see where and how community members live.

Receiving no encouragement for small talk, Martin silently assessed Karol while awaiting the directress. High cheekbones in a thin face, classy: must be a thoroughbred, he thought, nervous, difficult to control but providing rare satisfaction. He noted her faded blue serge suit's quality, the elegance she achieved by a spotted neckerchief. He could see her as a cool and competent antique-shop owner.

It was his lamentable bourgeois upbringing, he decided, which made him think of the directress as a tram driver as soon as she appeared. Short, robust, wearing a uniform-like grey suit, she had cropped auburn hair and a thick nose. Even though, fortyish, she must have been ten years younger than Karol, she was unquestionably in charge. Karol had to translate for the directress's only foreign language was Russian.

She said that during Martin's stay his hotel would be taken care of in payment for his story. "Our hotels are not expensive," she added, with either pride or humour. Martin wondered why the windows remained closed on such a stifling day.

Martin detected a quaver in Karol's voice as she translated the directress's assertion that Neruda had been transferred permanently from Prague. He took another cautious sip of the harsh brandy they had offered.

The directress requested Martin's help in translating other stories for the anthology. Martin reluctantly agreed to extend his stay and the directress offered Karol as a Prague guide. Mother superior letting her oldest novice off the leash, Martin judged, regretting that Karol was not twenty years younger. His protracted engagement with a Tuscan nurse had recently ended: she had married a doctor.

The directress, unwavering eye on Martin, concluded with a brief sermon on socialist regimes' cultural achievements compared with the supermarket mentality degrading capitalist culture. "Here we recognize writer's importance," was her refrain, "whereas in the West they're bought and sold." If someone had offered to buy me, Martin thought, I wouldn't be teaching spoiled brats in Rome. The directress extolled their program of publishing classics and selected contemporaries.

Working in Karol's cubicle, Martin found that her English was rusty. Even her portmanteau word for what she could not describe exactly, "thingamebob", seemed a relic from her last London visit. It became a joke between then. She admitted that French was her first translating language. But she did not explain why Ignat Neruda had abandoned what he had started. Martin, perched on a stool beside her small desk, felt the office was not the place to probe further.

Outside, however, she was not more forthcoming. They were at a restaurant where the napery, glassware and cutlery glistened but the food was anemic. Karol was charming: sophisticated and appreciative as if he were a renowned visiting writer. He enjoyed the tribute while knowing it was gained under false pretences as he had published, years ago, only one barely noticed collection of stories.

At one stage she said hopefully that he might write a Prague story.

"Don't believe in superficial travellers' tales."

She asked what he was writing.

"Just building up notes," he answered, pretending interest in the stringy Weiner Schnitzel, "don't believe in writers running something off their assembly line each year."

The obstacle evaded, conversation then ran swiftly until he asked her opinion of the regime. She became guarded. Martin was suddenly conscious of diners at nearby tables. Could they be eavesdropping, he asked imagining also that the slow, apparently distracted waiter might know more English than his thick "Yes sir, I'm sorry sir."

Karol apologized for the rocky pears served as dessert.

"Weather's been impossible — but you can't blame the regime for that, can you?"

"In Italy, people curse the government even when it rains."

"Here it rains a lot more," said Karol, straightfaced.

He tried to reopen the subject the following afternoon as they stood watching couples in rowboats drift on the broad, green-banked Ultava.

"Lovely," he exclaimed, wondering if she would

accept an invitation to take a boat with him, "I suppose it's the same as it was in the last century".

"I wasn't here." Her eyes were merry, soft-grey but luminous.

"What has changed though — anything improved?" He felt gauche.

A stooped man in a trench coat stopped within earshot and stood, a doused cigarette stub between his lips, looking at the boats. But it was not his presence, Martin felt, which made Karol fend him off again. Despite the watery sun, a sliver of cold sliced Martin's spine. He sneezed.

"Poor thing," Karol commiserated, "you can't wear the same clothes here as in Rome."

Martin had warmer clothes, but on arrival, had sent them to the hotel's laundry. Despite requests, they had not been returned.

"Let me take you to the National Museum," Karol suggested. She had decided, he was to realize, to educate him; it was in character as she, too, had been a teacher.

Although curious about Martin, his literary opinions and Italy, Karol was reticent about her own past. She came from a comfortable family of which she spoke with detachment. By travel pre-war, she had perfected several languages and become a languages teacher. She had married another teacher who was also a writer, a "cultural critic" she said proudly, who advocated wider cultural participation. And his widow, Martin deduced, was trying to provide culture for the masses in a way she thought her husband would approve. He gathered it was something of an effort for her.

Karol did not invite him home and continued to keep politics out of their conversation although, as they manoeuvred to avoid it, it was as palpable as an Ionesco corpse. Frequently Martin was drawn into a conversational minuet in which he felt obliged to half-praise aspects of Prague life. He presumed, for instance, that when he said walking was more pleasant than in Rome she realized it was because people could not afford cars. But she took it as a compliment.

Martin found himself trying to recapture exactly Karol's slightly stridulent voice. In anyone else, it would have grated on him. He caught the plea in it, unexpected from one so poised. She gave him two of her own illustrated books on historic Prague, she spared no trouble in searching for restaurants to please him. Eating with her, he sensed the possibility of a life in Prague. She became animated, grasping Martin's hand at the critical points, when she described her colleagues and provided an insight into the casuistry, the ideological scruples, the calculations involved in their publishing choices even though they avoided controversial contemporaries.

Martin submitted to Karol's didactic tours as he enjoyed her company despite the irksome conversational "off-limits". But the thought of them rankled as he lay in his melancholy hotel room after their National Museum visit.

On return, he had gone by mistake to the hotel's third floor instead of the second. In the corridor, a plainclothes standover man had demanded his passport. Apparently a Soviet delegation was lodged on that floor but this did not salve Martin's irritation.

On the second floor, Martin once again sought his laundry. The sultry arrival weather had given way to humid cold. Must have come with the Soviet delegation, he had told himself, while looking for the bell boy who usually sat reading, deaf to any callers, in a cubbyhole. Martin had paced the corridor, trying to still his shivering, for ten minutes before a silver-haired hotel employee appeared, displaying what Martin had come to think of as an authentic socialist sneer, common to those supposed to supply services. He knew nothing of the laundry. Martin retired to what he considered a perfect example of Czech hotel rooms as they were when he was born in 1929.

He reviewed the visit to the National Museum, a building which closed one end of broad Wenceslas square behind the good king's equestrian statue. Karol had been keen to explain its documents on the republic from its 1918 founding to the Communist's access to power, nineteen years ago, in 1948. But even without her amplifications, Martin found the documents eloquent testimony of Western powers' indifference and Germany's arrogance.

As they left, Karol told him that she had just returned from a language course in London when Neville Chamberlain had described Czechoslovakia as "the little country about which we know nothing". Of course she was right to be bitter, admitted Martin, switching on the bedside 1930s model radio, but he was still annoyed that she blacked out large areas from discussion.

A Radio Bucharest English-language newsreader said that during the week the Americans had dropped 1,000 tons of bombs on North Vietnam. Martin twiddled the dial until he heard jazz.

Karol implied that, as an outsider, he knew nothing of Czechoslovakia. He did not know much, Martin acknowledged, but a little more than the historical museum showed. He had read of the death of Jan Masaryk, foreign minister and son of the founding president Tomas G. Masaryk, shortly after the Communists took power: they had killed the only-begotten son of Czechoslovakia's creator. The same article noted that defenestration, Jan Masaryk's fate, was an old Czech custom. Seven Catholics had been tipped from a Prague window in the fifteenth century, which had started the Husite war, while the Thirty Years war began after four government officials were likewise defenestrated in 1618. Martin resolved to keep away from high windows in Prague, particularly on the hotel's third floor.

Prague pressed on him, confirming his initial intuition that it was tragic. He was learning more, he sensed, than Karol intended. She wanted to leave the Communist chapter unread, perhaps because she had a small part in its writing or because it was still unfinished. Or was it because she merely wanted him to know first what came before? He flicked off the radio and pulled the eiderdown around his shoulders for the night, finding warmth for the first time all day. He did not intend to take on Prague's woes, he had just dropped in.

Apparently Karol's lesson was finished but Martin started her off again. The defiant John Hus statue in the Old Town square prompted him to ask about other traces of Luther's forerunner, who was burnt at the stake. Karol took Martin through the narrow streets to the Bethlehem chapel. The interior was spacious and, after the city's baroque churches, refreshingly unadorned. A church built for the people, for an assembly, where Hus had lived and preached in the people's own language rather than in Rome-decreed Latin.

Hus had Martin's retrospective sympathy. Living in Rome made Martin aggressively Protestant. He had spasm of indignation at the Vatican, he occasionally launched into rigorist philippics against Italian attitudes but found life there too agreeable to persist.

"There's a Czech who didn't accept laws made thousands of miles away." He watched for her reaction.

Karol pulled up her old camel-hair overcoats' collar against the moist wind, but said only she would have to show him another religious figure. They returned to the Charles Bridge. Martin still in a paper-thin suit, miserably cold but curious. On the bridge, Karol craned to look at the dark, windruffled Ultava. Prague's colour, it came to Martin, was a glistening black-green like wet seaweed.

"That's where he finished," she nodded towards the water, then to the richly-fluted baroque statue at Martin's shoulder. He had to lean back to see the figure of a man with finger to his lips. Karol said it was St John Nepomuk: thrown to his watery death in 1393 by a king because, despite torture, he would not reveal what the queen had said in confession.

"We're very fond of him, he's Prague's patron." She gathered her black hair, which oldfashionedly was brushed behind her ears, in both hand in a satisfied gesture. Martin had to recognize her Nepomuk was a deft reply to his Hus. Silence, too, could be a form of resistance. Now he was enjoying her lessons.

The queen, she explained, was Bohemian. Of course, Martin recalled, they're Bohemians even if not exactly gay. And the king German. He wanted to ask if it would many any difference if he were Russian, say Ivan the Terrible, but then realized it had broken his dream.

He told Karol tht after their visit to the National Museum, he had dreamt that they were examining the wares of one of Prague's many side-walk medal-vendors. In fact, for some reason, Karol was as interested as the usually poorer customers in these medals and had stopped several times near Wenceslas square to examine them. In his dream, Martin had stood slightly apart for, as far as he was concerned, if you had seen one medal you'd seen them all. An old vendor, fixing him with pinpoint blue eyes, had pointed excitedly to his chest. "The Iron Cross," he had shouted, "first-class," although Martin could not tell whether with anger or just excitement. The others had turned on him in hatred; countless claws reached for him. He had woken, overheated, and thrown off the eiderdown.

"I'm always being taken for a German," Martin admitted. It was not surprising as he was six foot, fairheaded, blue-eyed.

"I'd never take you for one," protested Karol

loyally, "you've a different kind of fairness. Didn't I jump to your defence?"

"After taking me there," Martin teased, "you faded out of the picture. Silence," he said, tipping his head towards Nepomuk's statue, "is golden."

"But I've never left anyone in the lurch." Her tone was plangent and he realized he had been too facile. "You don't think I'd leave you like that?" she continued but indignantly.

Her intensity disconcerted him. Could she possibly believe it might happen?

"Of course not," he said, then switched back to the saint, "what sort of a name is that — Nepomuk?"

Karol explained that "Ne pomuk" meant "I will not talk". A wise monkey, thought Martin, who heard some evil but would not speak it.

"I'd prefer Hus any day . . ." he began but Karol had a finger to her chiselled lips. Her intelligent eyes spoke for her. The message was that, as he was beginning to understand, he should give himself a chance to think.

He agreed but his perceptions induced vertigo. For some reason, the Charles bridge reminded him that, during the darkest years of Czech political thuggery, a few of his older university contemporaries had worked in Prague for leftwing international student organizations. He was furious that they had not denounced the Czech tragedy. What could they have had in mind? Probably satisfied to have a job, board and lodgings like yourself came the answer.

He had stayed longer in Prague than anticipated because of Karol's good company and inadequate

English. But, apart from anything else, he feared he would contract pneumonia if he did not leave. He had acquired a permanent spinal cold spot. The night manager promised his laundry for the following day. On the strength of the promise, Martin washed his dirt-rimmed shirt in his room. As next morning his laundry still had not been returned, he had to stay in until his shirt dried, wrinkled but clean.

When he reached the office, he found Karol had brought him a brown sweater. It was canvas-hard and smelt of mothballs. But he was grateful for it when she took him later on a Kafka tour: the sky was bruised blue and the air coldedged.

He had known Kafka was from Prague. But the tour made him realize that Prague was Kafka's and his sinister castle the castle on the hill. Kafka had captured it all, the questions without the answers of the gothic, black-green, brooding city.

Karol showed him the Jewish cemetry and the memorial to Nazism's victims with names tightly packed from floor to ceiling. Many Kafkas.

"Did the Nazis kill him?" Martin asked, confused, for the city's strata on strata of horror seemed all one.

Karol, startled by the question, said Kafka had died in 1924.

"You're not Jewish are you? " he asked as they left.

"Do I look Jewish to you? "

"Can you really tell a Jew by sight? "

"People here can," she answered gravely.

"Your husband was a Jew," Martin asserted with an imaginative leap.

She nodded her head as if in silent satisfaction. It flashed on him that Karol, from a comfortable Catholic middle-class family, had jumped several ditches in her time to marry a leftist Jewish intellectual.

"And this is his sweater," he decided with another leap. Excited, he tugged at the sweater. Usually he examined his intuitions long enough to doubt them.

"I want you to keep it," commanded Karol, grasping him under the upper arm to pull him towards her. Like a comrade thought Martin, surprised. Her body was slim but not bony. Martin decided he would leave the next day.

That night, Karol took him to a magic-lantern theatre whose novel stage effects he admired. Theatre was irreplaceable in Prague, he saw, Karol was probably enjoying it just as her parents had. Prague's coffee bars, with newspapers clipped in cleft sticks available for clients, were likewise civilised except that the only papers available were Communist. For people such as Karol, the tradition still held he realized, catching another disturbing hint of a possible life in Prague. At intermission, she had to "retire to the ladies' room".

Martin was walking as fast as he could short of attracting attention, fleeing from her. He wanted only to be anywhere else, fast. She had trapped him, he felt, as if she were a spy assigned to shadow him from his first day in Prague.

But he had nowhere to go. At the first corner, he stopped by a sausage-vendor's stall. The sausage culture, he thought in his new role as cultural critic, begins at Innsbruck.

A car screeched around a far corner, its horn blaring at him as it whooshed past. He bent to see the bullnecked driver. The boot, above a German number plate, was packed with cardboard boxes. A German commercial traveller driving as if Czechoslovakia was his possession, Martin guessed, biting expectantly into a hot sausage. But, at the taste and sight of its interior, his chewing stopped. Grey, greasy, an obsecene mass of entrails. He spat out his mouthful as if it were wormladen, fit only for the Warsaw ghetto's last survivors. He felt he had crossed into an endlessly eastwards territory in which this porridge of intestines would be relished, where poverty was the only heritage and pogroms periodical.

His teeth chattered from the cold. At a hundred yards, the road faded because poorly-lit but the theatre foyer gilttered. Martin returned quickly and explained to Karol that he had stepped out for air.

Next morning, he recovered his laundry. Not by shouting, for he did not know how that would finish, but by stubbornly harassing the resentful staff. Finally, all his laundry was brought, the same bundle he had handed in on arrival, unwashed. The clothes had acquired a tannery smell.

"What's this? " shouted Martin, furious but knowing it was futile.

"Did not work, did not work" was the indifferent reply.

It put Martin in a snakey mood but he helped Karol through most of the remaining stories. At one stage, he found she did not know the meaning of "muddling through" and confused her further by using, as his example, her translating performance.

Then she asked why would a character "flog books". Martin explained that the character was not a sadist but was simply trying to sell review copies, then snapped at her for being as incompetent as the hotel staff.

"It needs someone used to contemporary idiom." Previously he had avoided rubbing it in.

"Some people fear we'll get too much practice at that," she said quietly and he was left wondering if it were a reference to herself or Neruda. Martin wanted to make amends.

As they walked to the station under sleety rain, she made a last apology for the weather. They passed a large bookstore, the only shop in the street whose window was illuminated. Hunched against the rain, Martin tried to share Karol's satisfaction over the rows of canonized books in their regimented jackets.

"In our cities," he consoled her, "you'd have to search for a bookshop in a bazaar of jewellers, boutiques, God-knows-what."

Thank God, he added silently, to be leaving a country where someone's highminded idea of culture was rammed down everybody's throat.

"Look Martin, look!" Excited, her voice took on a richer timbre. In the far corner, with what could have been a votive lamp before them, was a display of about thirty copies of the Czech version of Simenon's *Maigret in New York*. Although contemptuous of detective novels, Martin was delighted to see Karol radiant. She grasped his hand to pull him closer to the books.

"All your own work?" To his surprise, he recognized she was sexually attractive. I would, he told himself, when I'm on my way to the station.

And what a Mittel-European trap, he added, to find myself attracted to an older woman.

"No Martin, that's not the point. It's the first time he's been translated into Czech! "

Oh God, thought Martin, big deal. It made him even gladder to leave. He could imagine the dove-cot flurry when that audacious translation proposal had been made, the endless discussions as to whether it was opportune, the agonizing over the ideological aspects, the ultimate decision being left to Karol's boss, the crophaired commissar. Finally, the exciting news: the lucky Czechs were to be allowed to read Simenon. Martin felt exhausted thinking of it.

He had intended to put some blunt political questions to Karol at the station but now had no heart for them: they would only shadow her happiness. He reproved himself for churlishly wanting to examine her politics, for expecting her to share her past with him as if it was as uncomplicated as his own.

"I'll be a bit less like Neville Chamberlain," he promised as he stood with her on the platform.

She spread her arms wide, rendered inarticulate by emotion. She looked dowdy, old.

"His thingamebob, his brolly would come in handy though in this weather," Martin added, anxious not to leave her like that. What if she cried as the train pulled out?

He had to see her as happy again as she had been at the bookshop. He suggested he send her something from Rome, a scarf, a pair of gloves, Chianti because she had a discerning palate.

She pulled her old coat around her, narrowing

her eyes while assessing possibilities, then tossed her hair and asked, voice grating his skin like a nail, for paperback detective novels.

So much for *kulchur* thought Martin. The train was about to depart.

"Which authors? "

"Anything except *Maigret in New York* — we hardly see any here in Prague."

For the first time, he kissed her and felt her strong feminine hand on his neck pulling him towards her.

She did not follow the train but stood watching it, elbows clipped uncharacteristically close to her sides by her crossed hands.

In Rome, where Prague's pain was distant, he chose a dozen paperbacks Chandler, Agatha Christie, Ngaio Marsh, Highsmith, McBain and others.

In addition, he photocopied Hemingway's "Che ti dice la patria" which, after detailing the miserable spirit of Fascist Italy, concludes: "The whole trip had taken only ten days. Naturally, in such a short trip we had no opportunity to see how things were with the country or the people." Alongside this conclusion, Matin wrote that he had included the story in case a translation had never been made or a new one was needed.

It seemed clever at the time. But later, settled back in his teaching routine, he regretted he had not written to Karol himself instead of relying on Papa. He did not hear from her again even when Dubcek came to power, nor afterwards.

Heathen and Helot

THE ROOM WAS BARE: a grey concrete box in which the naked bulb revealed only a wooden bench and, against one wall, a crumpled mattress. A man in dirty khaki shorts slouched in, his head down. He had spent last night squeezed in a truck cabin. It had rained then; it was still raining. He put his bag on the bench, sat, and leant forward, elbows on his knees. His legs were hairless. A mild-looking man — pink face, spectacles and silver hair — who, although middle-aged, looked like a student, a small boy awaiting his headmaster.

A scrawled notice over the shower recess read "Welcome Boys! These rooms are yours! Keep them clean! " The man in khaki shorts did not notice. He was arched over, still seeing the white roadline slip, slip, winding into him until he felt he must vomit it. He concentrated on keeping his head firm between his hands, like a man attempting meditation under Kleig lights. He begged that the shaking cease, that his stomach stop churning. Already his jellied legs were steadier. He tried to ease his corded arms, to breathe deeply. A shower would flush him clean.

He slid a coin into the gas-meter, there was a click and he cranked its handle. But the water remained cold. He probed the antiquated mechanism with a nail file, then cranked, jerked, cranked angrily again until there was a rick, a judder and the handle would swing only backwards. He had spiked the hot-water system.

He sidled back to unroll three blankets. These rooms are yours. He felt the plump mattress but, under the bench, on the unyielding floor, lay instead on his own thin blankets. The room was stifling: a small, high window was the only break in its blind walls. He waited, unwashed, assured of his discomfort.

The door, bursting open, rebounded from the wall. Laurie stood against the rain and flashing sky, curly haired, eyes pockmarked with grease. With bitter emphasis, he read "Welcome Boys! These rooms are yours!" He slammed a bruised suitcase on the bench above the older man's head.

"How's the shower?"

"I'm going to wait til morning Laurie — too tired".

Laurie scattered clothes as he burrowed for a towel. Then, whistling "I'm nobody's sweetheart now", he entered the shower recess. The older man sat up, took Laurie's trousers and slid them between his blankets. The whistling broke off on a shrill peak.

"Some stupid galahs can't work a gas-meter without mucking it up."

"She busted Laurie?"

"Some stupid galah's managed to cruel it. Supposed to be fuckin fool-proof." Cockatoo-face's eyes glistened as, above the cold shower, Laurie bellowed sentimental songs. The older man liked Laurie's voice, the songs, the security. He dozed . . .

. . . He would turn on the cabin radio to drown the wheel-whine. Laurie's voice came, singing operatically "The Loveliest Night of the Year". The older man, incredulous, raised the volume. The voice swelled, then cut. The older man blinked his tight eyes to see the night road. Swing it over and roll, roll it back; swing it over and roll, roll it back. "Snakier than Marilyn Monroe eh? " chuckled the box-voice.

The older man stared at the toad-like radio's barred face. "S-bend! Jees! Don't you *see* those signs? Wake up, grandpa! You can't drive at night with maggoty eyes."

Silence, but it had to snap. What would the machine say next? Laurie's voice was low and lethal: "How long do you think you can bludge on me?

The older man twisted the radio's knob which came away in his hand. The voice bombarded him from all sides: "What'll you maul next? Talk about a motor mechaniac. And it would've been an idea to tighten the load before you started tonight. Don't want a Laurie-load smashed-up, do you? First sleep at that wheel's your last. Kerr-ist! Look where she's dragging, look out you silly old twat, keel her up . . ."

. . . He jumped awake. Thunder cracked outside like tarpauling loose on a load. He was glad of the room, the concrete box. Nothing to fear: there, drying himself and grinning, was the real Laurie, the great heathen. Good to see Laurie; marvellous build Laurie.

"Bad day eh, Laurie?"

"Bad as a woman. You bring the cushions in?"

"Thought you would".

"You silly old twat. I got to drive all day and be wet nurse at night?"

Laurie went into the rain, returning with two cushions. One smacked against the older man's face.

"Wet."

"Course it's wet. Everything's wet; shousing the cabin. No and I didn't fix it. Go out and fix it yourself if you want to."

The older man did not move.

"I hate the road Laurie."

It was a small whine, regretted as soon as spoken. Laurie straightened the mattress.

"God I hate it."

It had come again, like a prayer.

"You stupid twat. Half-tivoli this afternoon cause you can't hold the grog. I've pushed her through to here with two flats, and you trying to snore on me shoulder. You reckon *you've* had the road."

Laurie tipped his case off the bench.

"What'd you do if you wasn't on the road? God, what a weakie! Where'd you pick up your dumb mate, they say, the oldie? I've had some mates turn out no good but save me, Kerr-ist, I can't stand whingers. Save me from no-hoping whingers."

As Laurie gathered his case's contents, he banged boots and tins and the case itself against the wall and the bench, shaking red dust into the air. He came off his knees.

"You've got a hundred and ninety miles to do in the morning and you decide you're sick of the bloody road. I'll tell you what; I'll bore shit out of her for the hundred and ninety myself'".

He snapped off the light.

"I'll be rarin to do that hundred and ninety Laurie."

Laurie did not answer. He lay breathing evenly. "What time'll we set off Laurie?"

"When I wake up."

"What time do you want to wake?"

"When I've had enough shuteye. And I'm sick and tired of you waking me just when I'm starting to enjoy it. You can hang around until I'm ready. All right?"

"All right."

"Yair?"

"Yair."

"Apples?"

"Apples."

"Uh?"

"Uh."

The litany trailed off in grunts. The older man, who knew that hours would pass before he could sleep, lay thinking of Laurie waking, drowsy and mild; of sliding the trousers from between his thin blankets while Laurie searched for them in shower recess and truck. And the older man enjoyed in advance the great heathen's satisfaction on finding the trousers, just wherever he chose to put them.

Bangkok, Mon Amour

"THEY'RE TAKING a whiff of the breeze off the gutter," said Mrs. Harris as the long, shallow-bottomed launch passed a family seated on their porch despite the fetid smell which infested that part of the klong.

She put a handkerchief to her nose, "You could do worse in Redfern I suppose — *very* characteristic."

Lee Towers closed her ears. Recently her husband Ed had been a victim of cancer and she thought the East might assuage her loss but why, she asked, was she saddled with chirpy Mrs. Harris who could only see through narrowly Australian eyes? It had been bearable during the flight from Sydney and in their shared hotel room but on trips during the past three days it had proved infuriating.

Fortunately Les Fitchett, who sat on the other side of Lee, was entertaining himself with his camera for he was as Australia-anchored as Mrs. Harris. On the jet he had confounded the steward by asking for the sarsaparilla he habitually drank in Tasmania.

Lee, instead, relished the exotic. She peered into the open klong-side houses as if watching a strip illustration: in one the occupants were rising from sleeping mats, the occupants of others were washing in the river or eating from bowls against the background of photograph-packed walls: the King but not Queen Sirikit, others illustrious but unknown, and groups of . . . classmates?

A young couple sat watching builders at work on a house. "And spend the rest of their lives paying it off," was Mrs. Harris's knowing comment but Lee wanted to assert that here life was different. She found confirmation in the odd detail of a monkey which watched the watchers.

Opposite, a verandah stacked with coffins; at least they looked to be coffins but if the dead here were cremated there should be no need for them. Black strips of cloth hung from high poles in a dyer's. Black, she had read, was for working clothes and not for mourning. Change the colour of death, that appealed to Lee.

An old woman standing on a houseboat chewed vigorously then, as if she had haemorrhaged, retched out what seemed a stream of blood.

"Should have got that in glorious technicolour," drawled Les Fitchett.

"My God," exclaimed Mrs. Harris who did not recognize it was betel juice, "*charming.*" She looked for support from Lee but evidently she was in one of her glazed, see-no-evil moods. No children was Lee's problem, Mrs. Harris had decided. Carried a bit of a lance for the locals which might explain her wearing a sexy, too-young local caftan as her widow's weeds.

Women stood in the doorways surrounded by waving children. But at one door, watching the launch impassively, was a white man with a child in his arms. A Thai woman was seated on the floor near him hugging a smaller child. Lee's first thought was that he be a light-skinned Thai. It was unthinkable to find a white man here, particularly as these were quite the poorest group of huts on the klong. But no, he was stripped to the waist and the skin a singlet had protected was burnt redder than the rest.

Lee stood, grasped Mrs. Harris by the arm to draw her attention and told Les Fitchett to take a shot. He did so but, before they could understand why she had suddenly abandoned her haughty silence, the launch had glided too far for them to see clearly. Neither Mrs. Harris nor Les Fitchett could credit it was a white man.

"Albino Thai," suggested Mrs. Harris, "what would a white man be doing here?" "Must be a no-hoper," contributed Les, "what's it to you anyway?" Lee had no answer.

There was no point in trying to convince them but, shaken from her silence, she agreed with Mrs. Harris that the markdowns on the detergents and toothpastes visible in the canal-side stores were just what one found in Sydney. In one store, there was a blackboard on which was chalked

EAST WEST
HOME'S BEST

A shipyard, where high, broadbowed fishing boats, virginally white, were receiving the final touches, stood at the corner of a broader klong. Those in service, grey and businesslike, passed on their way to the Chao Paya Menam river, the children seated on their gunwales whitefaced from talcum powder applied to relieve prickly heat. But he did not have talcum on his chest, thought Lee, trying to remember if the children were white. She had no clear impression of them, they had seemed Thai.

They would become like the children who, from the banks, were hurling themselves into the water and swimming towards the launch, heedless of its propellor and laughing as they swallowed the wash. A girl, who had thoroughly soaped her younger brother and dunked him as the launch passed, smiled as if to illustrate the Thais-are-smiling-people cliche. Two boys about ten in natty swim trunks waited for the launch to draw level, jumped to grasp an overhanging branch, swung upwards Tarzan-style, then plummeted to the water. Would he see his sons perform like that, as much water babies as if they had grown in Sydney? It was possible to transplant, to cross the colour line, to find a new centre.

As the launch had reached the main current of the imperious Chao Paya Menam, it was a little easier to breathe. Les Fitchett had run out of film, Lee decided it was her last group excursion. Mrs. Harris cheerily summed-up: "It'll be a klong time before I want to smell another canal, *thanks muchly.*"

The roads were much longer than they looked on the map, the heat more insidious then Lee had realized. But she was happier, she was sure, than if trying to avoid Mrs. Harris while waiting for the bus to bring Les Fetchett and company from another hotel for their afternoon trip. She looked enviously at a pair of young blue-jeaned tourists who sauntered ahead. It was easy for them to pick-up the Eastern wavelength whereas she felt she had frittered away four days of her week's trip.

She wanted to check where she was on her map but the young woman crouched on the footpath beside a few pots of food (did they wheel out the remains of their lunch, Lee wanted to know, bemused by the modesty of these vendors who were found every few hundred yards) would be no help. She waited for a stroller who proved younger than his portly air suggested. She was looking for the river which, for her, made Bangkok something more than a sprawling, four-traffic-lane bedlam with huge hoardings and huge hotels, an ex R & R town where brothels, massage parlours and skinflick shows were cheek by groin. The young man said he was headed towards the river and would accompany her.

She was delighted to have made direct contact with a Thai instead of watching them from behind a bus window. He introduced himself (Petersoo was her approximation of his name), explaining that he was doing a master's degree in economics at the university which, Lee had not realized, flanked them. He had what she though of as an intelligent, Indian cast of features with a pronounced worry-furrow between his eyebrows. Darker than most Thais, he was very polite with good if stilted English.

To buy her a drink, he took her to one of the fry shops she would not have dared enter alone. She ordered the only drink she could see being consumed, Pepsi-cola, as did Petersoo who advised against the ice she requested, describing it as a health hazard.

Petersoo said he had visited Russia, Germany and Switzerland the previous summer. She liked his courteous manner, it seemed he was making a gentle offering when he spoke. He explained that his parents owned a coconut and pineapple farm at several house' train ride from Bangkok but they maintained a city house close to the university for him.

She did not tell him of her husband's death, as she did not want to make herself vulnerable, but confessed her interest in Eastern wisdom. Did she look odd to him, she wondered, in her bright caftan. A single white woman seeking what?

Never beautiful, she knew nearing fifty that she had worn well. She was tall (Petersoo came only to her shoulder), read widely, liked Chinese cooking, and felt on Ed's death that she had been atrociously tortured. It had made her want to flee Cremorne to find a future.

Despite her offer to do so, Petersoo paid for the Pepsis which reassured her. In the street again, where the heat once more wrapped her like a steam towel, she confided that morning's vision.

"You want to talk to that white man? " he asked, his brow furrowed deeper.

She had not realized it was possible but she did, she did.

Petersoo led her along narrow streets where cars competed directly with pedestrians, he guided her through a vegetable market, and finally brought her to the broad, loam-brown river. He commanded one of the waiting, rudimentary launches to back to the wharf.

"I hope this is not going to be expensive," said Lee with a smile to soften it. After buying the caftan, she found she barely had enough to last until departure on Tuesday. The trip, a last-minute decision, had been a strain on finances disorganized since her husband's death. Perhaps Petersoo would pay, or share expenses, as he was so well off. "Don't worry," he said and engaged in a lively exchange with the pilot.

She was surprised the launch stopped at the royal boat house where the king's gilded barges, shaped like legendary sea creatures, rode. Lee said she had seen them that morning but Petersoo continued to comment on sites as if he were a guide. "You're lucky to see things this way," he said, "with someone who lives here."

He did point out some new things: he identified a huge, enclosed villa as that of a Thai general, he indicated a group of river boats inhabited by Muslims, he showed her a pagoda partly hidden by trees. But she had thought he was a friend sharing her search, not a guide. She was upset and a little suspicious when she realized they were taking the longest way to the huts where she had spied the white man.

"What will this cost? " she asked sharply this time.

"Depends on his time," said Petersoo, "perhaps 300 bahts."

"Three hundred bahts! " More than the 250 bahts (about $10) for that morning's trip in a well-appointed launch. "Let's turn back."

"It's too late now." Still she had let Petersoo know, just in case he was in collusion with the pilot, that she was not a goldmine.

She forgot her fear of being fleeced, however, at the sight of the clutch of poor huts and houseboats where she had spotted the white man. They disembarked at the first hut to ask information and then slowly, with much palaver, visited them all. The longer it lasted, the more determined and frustrated Lee became. The white man could have been a phantasm. Petersoo turned often to her as if she should supply more details.

Apparently none knew of him although some, she was sure, were saying more than that. If only she could have pierced the language barrier, she was confident she would have drawn out a story. Petersoo remained cool and ineffective. Lee thought she recognized the white man's children and, perhaps, his wife. She tried a few English words on her without effect. What Lee identified as their house was occupied by old crones. Her parents? Did they hide him whenever other whites drew near?

"Don't you think one of these houses looks pretty much like another?" asked Petersoo as if he were slumming. She was bitterly disappointed. Petersoo expressed regret but she felt it was a formal sentiment which would have been appropriate to a government official.

They rode back in silence. As they neared the wharf, Lee urged him to beat the charge down to 100 bahts. After a brief discussion with the pilot on the wharf, Petersoo told her it was 400 bahts. Daylight robbery; Lee refused to pay. Petersoo said dispassionately she had wasted a lot of time looking for the white man.

Lee gave 200 bahts and Petersoo made up the difference, commenting that they should have bargained for the price beforehand.

As they left the wharf, she reproached herself for suspecting him. A temple complex stood nearby in ample grounds. Petersoo advised her against visiting it, saying that on Saturdays there was an admission fee whereas it would be free on Monday.

It sounded odd but she acquiesced. Had she been beastly over the launch? After all, she had offered to turn back and Petersoo was well-off. Four hundred bahts *was* exorbitant. She was not the normal tourist, rich and vacuous, and had not looked on him as a guide.

"I don't know how to ask this" Petersoo said quietly, "but I need 200 bahts until I can bring them to your hotel on Monday."

Saturday afternoon with banks, presumably, closed. She took two 100-baht notes from her purse without hesitation. She could not do otherwise as he had paid up like a gentleman. As a tough dame, she decided, she was an outright failure.

After taking her name, hotel, and room number, he put her in a taxi, bargaining with the driver to reduce the price to 20 bahts. Lee offered him a lift but he said he lived nearby.

It was only when the taxi passed the university, far from the wharf, that she remembered he had said his house was close to it. The launch trip surely could not have cost more than 100 bahts. She could imagine him, the smoothie, gloating over his success with his mate, the launch pilot, and recovering his 200 bahts from him.

Yet on Monday afternoon she awaited his call. On Sunday she had gone on the scheduled trip to Ayudhya with Mrs Harris, Les Fitchett and the merry group which made her hope, against all probability, that Petersoo would surface again on her second last day in Bangkok. She had thought of him on the last two nights, wondering if he always maintained his stately calm.

She whiled away her time reading the astrology column in the *Bangkok Post*. Mrs Harris lay sleeping on her bed like a fish out of water, the air-conditioner whirred like a jet engine, and Lee pored over a letter from a student signed simply P who, after giving a birth date, asked "if he would be able to travel from Thailand", if he would have a "fairly happy family" and a "somewhat secure financial future".

The phone rang: Petersoo from the reception desk. Lee dashed on eau de cologne and brushed her hair, black as any local's, reproving herself for her mean thoughts. What a bitch she had been about a few hundred bahts! It must have been the heat. And what a gentleman he had proved! No hope of learning anything from the East if she was uptight with miserable economies and petty suspicions.

She ran down the stairs like a young student. Petersoo met her with ceremonial grace. She led him to the bar, indifferent to the stares from the reception desk, and bought him a pepsi-cola.

It was not possible, he explained, to pay her back the 200 bahts today but as soon as his father transferred the money . . .

She reminded him of what he already knew: that she was leaving early the next day.

"Is there anything else I can do for you? " he asked softly, eyes full on her face but conveying that his thoughts were directed to her bedroom. There was no hint of a leer. A gentle offering with decorum maintained.

She was curious but the thought of Mrs Harris, gasping in panties and bra on the iodine-smelling sheets, was an effective deterrent. Although it would certainly take the chirp even out of Mrs H. if she awoke to find Petersoo in the flanking bed.

Did he make a business of this with female tourists? At 200 bahts a time?

"I'd like to see that temple," said Lee. Better at least than a group trip to the elephant pageant. He agreed. Probably relieved, thought Lee who felt she had a charming guide cheap. On the way, she questioned him about university students' political involvement. He disapproved.

The main stele in the temple complex, facing the Chao Paya, was intricately carved, with bent-kneed figures supporting successive bands of sculpture, and inlet elephant statues. It reminded Lee of photographs of Angkor Wat. Giant warriors, theatrically fierce, guarded a small temple in the pleasant grounds. Petersoo showed her the Buddhist monks' quarters, then led her into the main shrine's courtyard.

"You're very lucky," he told her, "this is open only a few days each year."

She wondered if he were boosting as he had on the klong trip. The temple courtyard was attractive as children played amid a series of saffron-sashed Buddhas and a row of Chinese equestrian statues.

There was an overflow crowd for a ceremony in the temple. Lee and Petersoo struggled up the packed steps until they could just see. As far as Lee could understand his explanation, it was a ceremony for civil servants who were to spend a period as monks.

The novices wore saffron robes whereas the officiating monk was in white. Baskets of elaborate gifts were ranged near the squatting monks. Overhead, a fan turned. The walls were painted with intricate blue landscapes. The ceremony was delightfully exotic, grave as the faces of the squatting onlookers but, Lee felt, lacking in awe. Then she saw the long glasses of reddish drinks which stood ready to be consumed: sarsaparilla, it seemed.

Petersoo was not merely boosting, it *was* something special. She would like to have lingered but felt an intruder and, besides, could not keep him waiting for her indefinitely.

She walked through the temple grounds again, grateful that Petersoo had brought her. She felt lighter than since her arrival or for a long time before. It was almost cool by the choppy river. There was a calm which compensated for the bittyness of her Bangkok days, the constant sticky heat, the loneliness she had felt in the tour group.

A vigorous fig tree, in which tinselly packages perched, was set deep in the grounds. Petersoo explained that it was the tree under which Buddha had received enlightenment. The packages were offerings from devotees.

Suddenly Lee was seated under the tree, claiming inner peace.

"If you had a camera I'd click you."

"There's too many of them on the trip already."

"It saves you money, anyway, not having one."

That was hostile, she registered, trying not to let it disturb her, I'm not really stingy. Couldn't he understand that some tourists left their cameras at home to seek an inner image?

"Inner peace comes only through renunciation of passion and desires," announced Petersoo as if he had achieved it.

I didn't renounce them, thought Lee, they were snatched from me with Ed's death. But you can burn through them too, she realized, otherwise you would end up floating like Petersoo.

"Where's your camera? " she asked, "I could take your picture."

She saw it then. He would come up white on the negative. And the white phantom on the klong would be black. If she had a camera, she would have left it in the fig tree, perched like a Brownie bird with hastily gathered flowers dying around it. She closed her eyes, training herself to see Petersoo, recapture the scene, her expanding peace when in Cremorne.

"I might visit your country. See how you manage your economy."

Better be quick, thought Lee. "Come and see me." He seemed uneasy that she was sitting under the tree even though the only other visitors were on the far side of the grounds. He kept looking over his shoulder as if he were stuck, it occured to her, with a silly old biddy who did not know her place. First a spurt of spite, now in a dither about decorum. She was glad a little of the real Petersoo was showing at last.

She rose reluctantly for, all of a sudden, she had found her way through, realized it is never exotic when you finally arrived.

This time he accepted her offer to share the taxi and left it near the university, but not before taking her Sydney address.

Lee had little time or money before departure but at a market near the hotel bought, for no apparent reason, a set of Thai baby clothes. Cheap, she told Mrs Harris loaded with silk, and she could give them to her late husband's secretary who was to marry. But she did not.

She bore the inevitable inconveniences of the departure better than others in the group. Some regretted that they were leaving, others that they had come at all. Lee, still wearing what Mrs Harris thought of as her call-girl caftan, had a new equability.

On the jet, Les Fitchett showed her the photograph taken in the klong; indistinct as if already blurred by distance, it showed no trace of a white man. Les had a tale to tell. Finding a Thai basket he had bought was too unwieldly, he had given it to one of his hotel's reception clerks who, in turn, had offered him his girlfriend for the night.

"Did you accept? " asked Lee.

"Cripes no," said Les, his eyebrows lifting at her cool question, "turn it up."

And he was not even sharing a room, she thought.

In her backgarden at Cremorne, Lee had a fig tree but she did not sit under it. Enlightenment had come in Bangkok. And, in any case, it was in her front garden that she saw at times her daemon lover, with a Thai child in his arms, looking impassively at ferry passengers as they glided beneath her house.

Memoirs of Catholic Boyhoods

Whelan's Complaint

I SLID THE SHUTTER closed for the night frustrated by the anonymity which is the strength of the confessional. Sometimes I feel the shutter is like a bank-teller's window. After it closes, he must draw up the day's balance sheet. I envy his dry accounting, for the spiritual one is more demanding.

But today, even more than usual, I regretted the conclusive slide of the wooden shutter which left me alone with my black-bound New Testament like a stone in my lap. I had wanted to talk at length with the last penitent who was such a laconic presence in the penumbra. I wished I could add a "berg" to my name, a psychiatry degree to my qualifications and as Clement Whelanberg invite him to tell me more from a comfortable couch.

Not many come now to confess they are bothered by Portnoy's complaint. It could be they are too busy hammering out what they hope will be a bestseller about it. But this admission, by itself, would have done anything but pique my interest. Rather it was his comment, which could have been flippant but instead was grateful, when I advised him to read St. Paul to the Romans: "should be better than cold showers".

For a second, I thought it could be Phil who had been in my thoughts since I took a walk the other day along the street where he used to live. I tried again to discern the features beyond the grate, waiting for Phil to chuckle and declare himself. But then I decided Phil would not go to such lengths to amuse, embarrass or punish me. Presumably he was over his desire to confess to me.

But there was another reason I was anxious to help. From what he said, it was clear the penitent was married. I saw his complaint as symptom of a conflict more worrying than if he had been a adolescent. However as he was disinclined to talk, I dried up. He seemed ashamed to say much more. Confession-shy, and I could offer little more than absolution, hoping he would open out more if he returned. It made me wonder if Phil was plagued by the same problem. And I could not help thinking how I had unwittingly provoked his initial addiction through what amounted to impatience.

To avoid misunderstanding, I should say at once that I had been as interested as Phil in girls. But my tactics had differed from his. My approaches were like guerrilla raids, abrupt confrontations. For instance, I followed a smouldering Jewish girl, who had a reputation as a "good catholic sort", along Alma Road and into her white brick house handy to the Temple Beth'Israel. Her mother was in the entrance hall but coolly I asked if she would summon her daughter. When she came, the conversation was inconsequential.

There was Lynette who I had met at a dance at the convent opposite our school and who, chance would have it, was a tennis opponent of Phil's Nina.

Whereas Nina was the slim, sporting type, flamehaired Lynette's burgeoning breasts, although forewarning she would become matronly, at that time were magnetic. Lying in wait after school, I confronted her several times in the street near her house but she never heard the undertones, the implications in my conversation.

Nevertheless Phil liked to pretend there was something between Lynette and me even if only as a pretext for talking about Nina. We spent countless hours on the subject. As his street came first on the way home from school, he would drop his Gladstone bag and begin, perhaps, with a rehearsal of their last conversation, adding all possible interpretations of the goddess's delphic words. Equally it might have been with jazz records in the background at his grandparents' two-storied wooden house, for they raised him, or at my house or wandering endlessly through St. Kilda and Malvern, over the phone, or even in company whenever Phil found the conversation did not divert him.

In company, and often out of it, he referred to the Holt family in code. Nina became Banana because he had first been ravished by her beauty when he saw her choosing a bunch of bananas at the Orrong Road greengrocer's. Her elder sister Annette was given the self-explanatory nickname Hoyden. Her socially ambitious mother was Bonbons which had to be read backwards like the legend on our neighbour's gate Emo Hruo; and her doctor father was called Snarl.

These pseudonyms were inserted in our habitual numerical code, running from 1 to 64, which Phil had invented mainly to flash messages across the classroom. Two, for instance, stood for something funny; four for a strange noise such as a Chinese market gardener's cart squeaking alongside the school which would send our maths teacher beserk; nine meant a bore such as the uplifting lectures we occasionally received from upright, uptight citizens; 31 "look at Noel Dando" and so on. There were also a few coinages such as "boyoyoy" meaning embarrassment.

Perhaps we had been trapped into afternoon tea with my mother and sisters. Phil would intersperse, when my mother paused for breath, "Terrible nine, tell you twoish Bonbons" which translated "This is a bore, I want to tell you something funny about Mrs. Holt." It is a simple example of a code which normally was more complex as in "Had boyboyoys with Bonbons over twoish remark by Snarl after their bloody cur's combined 4-27."

I could not keep up with him all the time, partly because , although I gave an impression of interest, my mind was elsewhere because nothing much happened between him and Banana. I had understood promptly that Lynette did not want to decode my messages but Phil went on for months, it was more than a year now, mooning over Banana without making progress.

"What do you make of it Clem, old horse?" he would ask occasionally when his hopes dropped, "got me bushed — but not yet in the burning one."

I had no satisfying answer anymore than when he asked me every now and again how many times married couples did it weekly. "Once, twice?" he asked as if it deserved intense study, "Don Iddon says an American survey shows those under 40 are at it three times a week — how'd you be?"

I considered his relationship with Banana the dullest aspect of my most congenial friend. His speciality was pulling atrocious faces or staging madcap scenes when teachers were writing on the blackboard and assuming a mask of compunction when they turned to bawl at those they found writhed in laughter. He also drew monstrous, pained creatures like his horrific faces as if he were acting out some suffering, but I gave this only fleeting consideration. He was a swift punster. He had read all Dickens and in the park beside school became the bizarre characters with an immersion which would have credited Emlyn Williams. To add to his sophistication when speaking French he would raise an eyebrow like Claude Rains. He had a childish fear of fights and a refreshingly complete incompetence in sport although echoing its catch words: "South got beat on the wing." "That Vic Patrick — couldn't fight his way out of a paper bag."

My parents warmed to Phil. I think they saw him as persistently boyish, even though he could be as formal as an old-fashioned gentleman for brief periods usually terminated by heroic laughter. He might have been surreptitiously smoking my father's cigarettes or drinking port from his cut-crystal decanter when my mother returned from shopping but she could not distinguish his loosened laughter from his normal guffaws. And was charmed by the old-world air he affected when really unsure of his stability.

This occurred with increasing frequency as he

gradually realized he was no nearer than a year before to peeling Banana. And classmates, who had been slower off the mark, were scoring squalid successes at the milkbar by Windsor station. Our biological alarm clocks go off unexpectedly to jar us awake. Phil's and mine had gone off early but I had dozed again. However others were being trilled awake. Kingham reported on the couch copulations he could see next door when he retired to write at night in a small attic. A bonus that would keep him at it for years. Phil ground his teeth in envy as he listened to Kingham's blushing reports. Arthur, a future doctor, began to talk knowingly of menstrual cycles.

We had to arrange for Phil to be alone with Banana in favourable circumstances. He was constrained by the antiseptic politeness which reigned at Snarl's Malvern mansion. It was unthinkable that he take her to his grandparents. Occasionally he accompanied her to the local Catholic tennis club but was at a disadvantage there where they would hardly see the humor in talk about South being beat on the wing. Cinema and concerts remained stilted. Walks were for the exclusive benefit of Banana's neurotic wirehaired terrier. Finally I came to the rescue by offering him our house for an afternoon.

Rarely were my parents and elder brother all away but he was upcountry fruitpicking and they had been invited to a wedding. Phil told Banana that, as I was playing pingpong with Lynette and others, they could drop in. They found an empty house and a note saying I had gone to collect Lynette. Instead I was loitering in a park nearby with my eye on the house of a friend who had driven my parents to the wedding. He would drive them back to his place, for a ritual visit to his bedridden mother, before accompanying them home.

After Phil and Banana had been in the house a while, I rang to ask how he was faring. For the occasion, he adopted the vulgate: "Bottler" came his reply. I suggested facetiously that he might want to fill in his time playing table tennis. "Got no balls" he said with a rumbling laugh "poorly equipped for a gymkhana but you run to good port. My mistress awaits me" he whispered with simulated heavy breathing, then hung up. It had worked. If Banana had been encouraging in more difficult circumstances, here surely she should finally recognize Phil's endowments.

I thought of walking to Lynette's and bearding her in her house. Perhaps finding her alone I could make her understand what I did not myself. Her skin looked irradiated by an inner light; how could she be so impervious to me? I rang but there was no answer.

Scorching sun, high sky. A cricket match was in progress. The only interest was in a quickeyed, left-handed slogger but when he skied a catch I tried Lynette's number again without success.

I wondered what stage Phil and Banana had reached. Would Phil sing in time with his jazz records that I had brought to the house in preparation for the afternoon? He could scarcely use his numerical code as it would be doubledutch to Banana. What would she make of Dickens imitations? Although I had met her only once, after Mass, she did not seem the type who would swap puns. Feline but not playful. Most limiting of all, he could not spend his time with her plotting all her possible moves and motives. I realized Banana had become a large part of the link between us. But with Banana, that talk would have to come to a halt. I couldn't hear them at all. What could you talk about with girls for any length of time anyway? Of course there was action, which was what Phil was after, but how that was managed, in its ultimate phases, was a mystery. At least I had provided Phil a splendid opportunity to plumb it.

My reverie was broken when I saw my parents in the drive-way of their friends' house. The car had arrived without my noticing, probably because it was much earlier than expected. I felt prickly. I had told Phil he need not think about leaving for an hour yet. But I knew my parents would make a perfunctory visit and could be home in a matter of minutes.

I ran Alma Road faster than I had ever done in my daily training for the school sports. There were no short cuts and no alternative routes home as East St. Kilda cemetery occupied a whole block. If my parents did little more than walk in and out of their friends' house, as would be my father's intention, the car bringing them home would overtake me. I developed an early stitch but I hoped that, in time, it would save boyoyoys.

When I reached home the car was still not in sight. Phil, sitting alone by the gramophone, could have been a meditative statue, a stunned mullet. I must have expected him to be euphoric because the sight jolted me. I asked how it had gone. "Nine" was the deeptoned response as if I had disturbed profound thoughts.

A fug of stale tobacco, the port decanter empty, a record scratching on aimlessly.

"Didn't you hear Buddy Bolden shout?" I asked, opening the window.

A grunt was his only response to the allusion.

"Where's mater keep the Aspros she's always taking?" he asked abstractedly, "Banana's gone to look for them. She's got a bad head."

"Get her out: Mum and Dad will be here in a few minutes."

He seemed incapable of movement.

"Slam us together, then cast us into the outer darkness. P's sick of the wedding? Never understood what people see in 'em."

Banana returned. Talking about her almost daily had been inadequate preparation for having her in our front room in all her blonde, baby-faced femininity. And bad-tempered.

"Thanks for the pingpong afternoon. Terrific! Can't tell you how much I enjoyed it. Guess Lynette couldn't stand the pong."

Small features puffy with annoyance, her tone as self-righteous as her mother's. I had to tell her I was delayed because Lynette had had an accident.

The important thing was to get them out and put the room in order before my parents arrived. Previously Phil had taken only a few cigarettes at a time and at most a glass or two of port. Now two cigarette packets were empty as was the port decanter which had been half-full. Cigarette butts lay on the Axminster.

Although Phil was slow and truculent; he moved Banana in the right direction. He was almost as testy with me as she had been which I took as a shrewd way of ensuring she left swiftly. For while she may have had her reasons, as she had been invited on false pretences, surely he should only have been grateful.

Something had gone wrong. But I felt blameless and that they wanted to make a convenient scape-goat. At any time, I was impatient with complexity, but particularly now when I could not lose precious seconds weighing motives. Once they were out the door, I put the living room in order. My father kept a stock of cigarettes in his cabinet and I was able to replace those which had been smoked. There was no more port for the decanter but I put that away in the sideboard as he took it out only when we had guests.

The smoke hung like a drape as it was an airless afternoon but I opened the back door as well as the front to create a draught. I even had time to put back my mother's pharmacy which Banana had strewn in her search for Aspro.

My parents noticed nothing. It was only the following day that my mother questioned me about the afternoon. Before answering, I found that Bonbons had rung, indignant that her daughter had returned from our house reeking of alcohol. It seemed she thought I was trying to seduce Banana.

That possibility rather intrigued my mother who was jealous of the Holts. But she was disappointed by my deception the previous afternoon. If Banana had thrown her mother off the track so cutely, I could only keep up the good work. After all, my mother found Phil such a nice boy and the truth was more complicated than fiction. I told her Banana had come to play pingpong, that she had drunk a little port and the decanter had tipped over. I did not mention the cigarettes and bought others to replace those taken from my father's cabinet. My mother ordered port to replenish the decanter.

In a sense, it all ended there. When I rang Phil some hours after he had left precipitiously with Banana he was, for the first time, taciturn and we never quite recovered our complete, preassignation camaraderie. I was exultant that I had covered their tracks but he was flat. I asked whether, in responding to my query as to his success, he had intended "nine" in our code, signifying boredom, or "nine" on the sexual scorecard which, although I was not sure what it meant, was nearest to the unimaginable initiation. After a pause, he answered "Both". It was not altogether convincing but he was disinclined to elaborate. Presuming he was tired, I let him go and remained a little baffled.

He brightened when I told him next evening that Banana had protected him after her mother had found she had been drinking. But although he maintained the pretence for a while, he did not believe in the affair any more. He saw Banana every now and again but was cured.

Next, however, he contracted Portnoy's complaint. He confessed regularly and then reported the confession, word for word, question and answer, to me.

He was incredulous when, in response to his query, I said I did not indulge.

"Lynette looking after you, eh?" he suggested with a wink although he knew I had not seen Lynette for months.

"Don't know how you do it Clem, old son," he continued, "or rather don't do it. Armed with the faith? Good apple, bad basket. Cold showers are the shot anyway," he said, sighing as he repeated his confessor's ineffectual advice. He had been taking them for years.

They were no antidote: what had begun as a guilty infraction threatened to end as a cause for boasting. It really had been less boring to hear about the Holts but he persisted in his accounts as if I owed him a hearing. I told him his reports were a nine but he said there were worse ones. He was the man who drove out one devil only to be invaded by nine.

I had a quiver of interests whether in the back-yard broadcasting Test matches in which I was a protagonist or training for the school mile race or reading Shaw's complete plays or exploring Catholic thinkers who seemed to have plumbed the universe's height and breadth and depth. Life was no nine but I wanted to do something generous with mine. After a year or so I entered a seminary. I don't regret it even if I soon found my limits to the height, the breadth and the depth.

What I had not foreseen were the long hours I would have to spend in the confessional in my central city church. Central city sluice as Kingham calls it. You hear a lot about confessions falling off but I have hordes with a high proportion of regulars.

I do what I can, especially in trying to ease the straitjacket of scrupulosity some stitch on themselves. Many just need someone to listen and patience is the best help you can give. Patience, rather than passivity, was something I began to learn from my experience with Phil. But don't imagine this is a tale wagged by its moral. Please don't jump to the conclusion that a boyhood trauma drove me into a confessional for the rest of my life. Leave such sledgehammer simplifications to "True Confessions".

If you're interested, Phil and Banana are married although not to each other. Banana to a doctor who, wait for it, was assistant to her daddy. They live in North Balwyn within striking distance of the p's. Unsnarl that one for yourself. Phil is living in another city, married with kids, a stout Catholic, once a sinner but never a rebel.

Only the other day I walked down the street where he used to live twenty-five years ago, a quarter of a century already. Narrower than I remembered it and with not much unchanged. Where his grandparents' wooden house stood, there is a block of unit flats, anonymous, and a private hospital. Is it possible that over a hundred people are packed into the space once adequate only for Phil, his grandparents and the aunt who, he claimed, was the unwitting cause of his first erection when he slept with her at the age of five.

The street stretches to infinity in its sameness. A girl was walking in that desert, nothing special but fresh, free, burgeoning. In such a setting, I recognized, such a girl could be your Beatrice if you didn't try to crack the code too quickly. Dante had only seen her fleetingly and look what a web he spun. Way of keeping himself at halfmast, Kingham would say. But I saw it was a way of picking up the thread, tracing the cabal of continuity.

It came back to me hów annoyed Phil and Banana had been when I stagemanaged their confrontation. And with it, the reason. Face to face without constraints, Phil and Banana had realized that she rated nine on our arcane points system. There were no thanks to the matchmaker for destroying their illusions.

It has taken me a long time to understand that as with other things I thought I had sewn up years ago. Now it can only remain as pure knowledge, useless. As I said, biological clocks are unpredictable and even when they ring one can fall asleep again for years. After listening constantly to so many tales, for a change you sometimes feel like telling one yourself, just one.

Invincible Ignorance

DAN FELT HIS SPIRIT   liberated beyond the confines of the Xavier College classroom as Father Riordan spoke, his forehead luminous under his prematurely silver hair. With a beatific smile, Riordan was saying that Luther, Calvin and Cromwell could all be in heaven. His words made history a struggle of blind men all serving God. But if only the blindfolds could be removed, Dan decided, they would recognize each other as brothers.

He tried our Riordan's words on his mother at dinner that evening to interrupt a dirge about her boss in the legal office, Mr Blunden. He wanted to illuminate the prim, spinsterly kitchen, to suggest she could be free.

"Mr Blunden's probably doing the best by his lights — could go to heaven like a shot!" Mrs Donellan's forehead knitted tighter for she heard an echo of her own ardour before faith became an armature.

"Luther", Dan went on, wondering why his mother could not take off her hat before serving dinner, "and Calvin - probably enjoying the beatific vision by this time."

"I didn't send you to Xavier," Mrs Donellan said, irritated because Mr Blunden was problem enough, "to get ideas like that." Rather to equip him for the legal career her husband Eric had abandoned when he vanished.

"It's the intentions that count. Even Cromwell could have been righteous."

It was too much. What was the point of scraping and saving to send him to Xavier if they taught him all cats were grey? She wanted him as rigidly Catholic as she had become since her mixed marriage had broken up. And qualified to excel in a world where Masons and Jews looked after their own. She nurtured memories of seeking jobs during the Depression, when owning-up to Catholicism was a disqualification. She could never pass a certain Collins Street jeweller without a smart of indignation at being refused a job because of her religion."Invincible ignorance — that's the term, isn't it?" she said as if she had found the answer. "They might be saved because they couldn't see the light."

The blindness of Eric her husband, of Blunden, was that of Cromwell, Calvin and Luther. "But couldn't is often wouldn't," she added severely.

He was sorry she could not get beyond her bitterness. But he was wary of disclosing his vision of universal brotherhood in case she scoffed at it. She had blighted other enthusiasms, for example lamenting there was no money for stamps or horseriding. Now, at fourteen, he suspected this was due more to habit than necessity.

"How could they if the Catholics about them were so opaque?"

"You're not a pane of glass yourself," she wagged her knife at him didactically, "when you're pummeling Reg Howard."

Reg Howard, a reedy, strawhaired boy a year older than Dan, was the son of a Communist schoolteacher neighbor. Despite Russia being a valiant ally against the Axis, the Howards were still curiosities in that corner of St Kilda. Reg baited Dan on attending Xavier and they squabbled and scrapped, using their elders' arguments, over Church and Party.

"Everyone gets his deserts eventually," said Mrs Donellan, passing Dan his stewed rhubarb. "Let God worry about intentions." It was a mistake to be flurried, she decided. It would be a passing phase like acne and his exaltation after spiritual retreats. With time, he would learn that life was different from fine words.

Most weekends, Dan escaped to his grandparents. He decided to try out the good news on them

"Nobody ever said there's not good people of other faiths," said his grandmother, offering Dan her flat fruitcake which he always associated with her, "but there's only one true faith and your forebears suffered for it." She did not mention his immediate forebear. There was a family fear that Dan may have inherited his father's irresponsibility as well as his sultry looks.

"Go on, young fellow," his grandfather, encouraged Dan when he sketched the idea of heaven populated by Luther, Calvin and Cromwell. "The devil too," added his grandfather, shrunken like a tough brown nut, bent over carving wood, which was his consolation during retirement. "Old Nick's more likely to get a final reprieve than Cromwell. Have to draw the line somewhere."

Years ago, Dan recalled, his grandfather had shown him a thick volume bound in red leather and told him it was a theological treatise. He kept it in his wardrobe which he ceremoniously locked after taking anything out of it. This intrigued Dan and added to the mystery of that book which he had thought of as some kind of cabala. He asked what it had to say on the subject.

"I don't know about that," said his grandfather slowly for he was in a difficult phase of the carving. "It's not easy to follow." He look at Dan, his steel-rimmed spectacles at midpoint of his straight nose, "But there's a lot more to it than *we're* told."

Dan intended to act on his knowledge. He would cease swapping blows and abuse with Reg Howard. There had been periods of tolerance between their slinging matches. Now Dan would listen to what Reg was saying. He began to frequent the Howards' house which was paint-starved as if in reproof to the houseproud neighbors.

Reg, after an initial gawky diffidence at Dan's new style, proudly showed him has father's Marxist library and was impatient when Lucy, his sister who was two years younger, harassed them for help with her homework. Dan found the blue-bound volumes of Lenin's works, which he had expected to be exciting, formidably dull.

Mrs Donellan, returning from her tiring day as secretary to Mr Blunden, was dismayed to find ever more frequently that Dan was at the Howards'. As a sallow spring followed Melbourne's rigid winter without Dan coming to his senses, she sought the parish priest's aid.

"You would insist on sending him to Xavier rather than the Christian Brothers," said Father Meehan slyly, the pale sun making his creased face like weathered sandstone. Dan was relieved the priest did not take his mother too seriously for he was just discerning a horizon beyond hers. Father Meehan gave Dan books in case he had to handle Howard senior and told Mrs Donellan the Jesuits were used to preparing missionaries.

That did nothing to console her. Her anxiety made her nag Dan inconsequentially when he brought home pamphlets against international capitalism or went to special showings of Soviet films. She much preferred the days when her worry while returning home had been that she would find him hurt from fighting the Howard boy. Father Riordan, she repeated doggedly, has a lot to answer for.

But the impetus Father Riordan imparted would have died by this time if Dan had not found his own momentum. The Howards attracted him because they dreamed of shaping a new world, instead of being shaped by the existing one, as his mother proposed.

Reg accompanied his father on a visit to an ailing brother on a soldier settlement farm near Mildura. And in Reg's absence Lucy insisted on continuing his half of the album he was compiling with Dan. This consisted of examples of social injustice clipped from the papers. Alternately Reg and Dan supplied the example and had to match it with comments drawn from Christian or Marxist texts, plus an analysis of causes and suggestions for remedies.

Dan had proposed the idea because Father Riordan had his class working on it. Reg took to it keenly but was unimpressed by the quotes which Dan had believed were incisive. Reg wanted analysis of economic factors. Even though Reg's analyses were always more or less the same, Dan suspected he had help from his father.

Lucy, who was flaxen-haired and as thin as Reg, set a different style. Reg emphasized the big international injustices which he attributed to the machinations of monopoly capitalism. Lucy went for cases of individual misfortune: mother of eight refused entry to a hospital, pensioner asked to leave boarding house, children suffering malnutrition.

She was weak on quotations and analysis. "Someone should help these poor bathplugs," she wrote beside her first item and "ditto" beside the second. However, she like pasting photographs in the album even if they barely related to the items. Dan was warmed by her ready sympathy for all victims. She was generous also in bringing him long glasses of lemonade.

On his return, Reg took the updated album as a breach of trust. Women were given little importance in the Howard household. For him, Lucy's selections were proof positive of her inability to see beyond details.

"An easy way for you to look good," he said, even more redfaced than the Mildura sun had made him, as he slammed the album on the table in front of Dan.

"I thought they were lively," Dan answered, deciding not to add Lucy's items were a welcome change after Reg's monotonous contributions.

"A silly bloody game anyway," said Reg sulkily, "suitable for kids like you and Lucy."

Dan felt embarrassed as well as resentful.

"Cutting up newspapers is not going to change anything. You should see the slice of desert they gave my uncle to farm."

Everyone gets the desert he deserves, thought Dan savagely as he shook the album of clippings into order. He could not be held responsible for the miseries of Reg's uncle. "I'll take this anyway," he said, outwardly calm, "if you're not interested."

"Better leave it here than have Xavier snobs pawing over it," said Reg.

He made a grab for it. It was a reflex for Dan to sway aside and tip Reg over as he followed through. But Reg was determined to get the album and caught Dan before he reached the front gate. They fought as if to make up for the scraps they had missed in the long months of understanding. Reg was taller and more violent although Dan was now stronger. But they stopped in midcourse, shamefaced, wondering why they were hating each other. The album, which both of them hated now, had finished in shreds. Each of them clasped tatters of human miseries comforted only by peremptory quotations and perfunctory analyses.

As Mrs Donellan bathed Dan's swollen lips and bruised eye that night, she commiserated with him. But he understood she was overjoyed that he had girded again the warrior's sword. While washing the dinner dishes, she told Dan contentedly that in this world it was a matter of fighting the good fight. It went without saying that she was confident about the destination of Eric and Mr Blunden, Masons and Jews and Communists as well as Luther and Calvin and Cromwell in the next.

She had known that Dan could not live off fine words alone. Indeed the world of pure and distinct ideas had died for Dan. Mrs Donellan would have understood if she had not been as invincibly ignorant of her son as she had been of his father.

He allowed his mother her content that night for he had begun to sense that, while men could all be brothers, the piquancy derived from the fact that they had sisters.

Yours Sincerly

"THEY WERE JEHOVAH WITNESSES," said my wife, between amusement and annoyance, when she came from the door, "warning that you never know when He's coming. Told them I was a Buddhist."

She had an air of "as-if-I-didn't-have-enough-to-do." My daughter wanted to know what Witnesses were. When my wife said they would not allow transfusions even when children are dying, it excited her interest further.

I asked if they had left any pamphlets.

"Who'd want them?" said my wife. On her way to the kitchen she began to answer my daughter's anxious questions. Who'd want them? I would. I could see the slim pamphlets, poorly printed, with the biblical quotes perhaps in red — impelling, incandescent. I imagined the Witnesses as carrot-haired, gawky, afflicted by adolescent acne despite adulthood, eyes glazed with the fervour of a belief which I regarded, momentarily, with nostalgic envy.

Once I too had awaited — no invoked — the Second Coming. I knew the longing of those who expect the Lord to unmask hypocrites, humble the mighty, and separate the just from the unjust.

I had toyed with the idea of the judgment day for some time before I seized on it like a sword. An old aunt's words, "It's not the dying but the judgment which worries me". had embedded themselves deep; but what I relished was the theatrical end-of-the-world bit, the angels trumpeting the arrival of the Lord in a magnesium-flash of majesty. The end-of-the-world appealed as the last laugh on quotidianity: you could not get too sunk into your part to forget that at any minute the painted scene might be whipped away.

I could not remember who first spoke of the judgment day to us: awareness seemed to be planted like those seeds which sprout only after a scorching fire. It could not have been Father Curtin, at the church which adjoined the school, as he was more likely to talk of second innings than of the Second Coming. It may have been the Brothers, but they were more intent on conveying a version of the beyond inherited from distant Ireland: not leprechauns but stories such as that of a headmaster passing outside third-floor classrooms, on the side of a building with a sheer drop to the ground, fifteen years after his death. Intended to fill us with awe for the prodigies of the holy, it chilled us with the hint that the beyond was a vast Brothers' school. The Irish-beyond counselled caution but the Irish-past nourished a desire for justice even if in terms of comeuppance. Assigned a three-page essay on a topic of my choice, I had turned in a twenty-five page dirge inspired by Ireland's wrongs. But the scorching fire which caused the seeds to sprout was ignited by Brother Whacker Wallace rather than by mulling over the Black and Tans' misdeeds.

Wallace wanted to denounce me to my father on his return from a trip to Sydney. Although my father and I were a pair both physically (slim, long-faced, with crinkly sandy hair) and psychologically (determined, proud), I feared he might believe Wallace's distortions because of his profound respect for the Brothers. But I knew I was justified before heaven. I prayed that the skies split open the Friday my father was to see Wallace, revealing his true colors.

I had been rigid with righteousness when I had challenged Wallace. Beginning of drawing class: as usual, Wallace, boisterous philistine, had asked our art teacher Holditch to hand over for a moment. "You chaps are free, of course, to sketch and etch but if you'd devote five minutes to addressing these envelopes, you'd help bring the faith to those born without it."

Holditch standing aside, smiling as if it hurt, one hand exploring the back of the hair which we swore was a wig. Two strikes against him: a layman and an art teacher. Any layman teaching in a Brothers school was suspect of a murky background ranging from a lack of proper qualifications to unspeakable practices which would exclude him from the State circuit. Holditch was shaky on several counts. He was a kind of cut-price Beau Brummel, a bachelor who on weekends cruised the bayside suburbs in an old, white MG. He taught meticulously but with a resigned detachment, perhaps because art teaching was considered the refuge of the limp-wristed and art classes as fatuous as our earlier singing or elocution lessons. The Barcarole, Tit Willow . . .

Although Holditch wilted before Wallace, one true artist set about his work while the remainder of the class happily addressed begging letters. They were not inspirited by zeal for the heathens Wallace's brother was converting in the Solomons but by the opportunity to skip drawing and keep on the right side of Whacker.

They were five minutes, usually going on fifteen, which Wallace regularly stole from the art class. A quarter of an hour of badinage between Wallace and the boys as he waived the rule of silence which prevailed in his own classes.

That day, however, the noise gradually decreased until I felt I was drawing isolated on a dais. I fenced out the uncanny silence as I wanted to pin Wallace to his words. Also I enjoyed showing I was different. I was determined to prove it further by not marrying nor drinking nor smoking nor falling into any of the drab compromises which I saw around me.

When I looked up, Wallace was standing close by, hands on hips. His brushed-back black hair seemed to stand up, his eyes behind his black-rimmed spectacles were owlish, a pallor appeared under his tan. "Well done Corcoran," he said, small-voiced between tight lips, "later you must show me your masterpiece which is so much more important than helping those without the faith."

Finesse, however, was not his forte. The explosion came towards the end of the following geography class during which Wallace had ignored me. A prefect entered to hand him a slip of paper which he read to the class: "Hehir and Corcoran have been selected to play for the first eleven in the match which begins at two tomorrow."

We were the youngest pair to have been selected for the team.

"Don't tell me you want sonky Corcoran!"

"Could be our best all-rounder," was the answer from the prefect who could not credit blatant antipathy. Perhaps he did not know that Wallace was never among the Brothers who stopped at the school nets to admire my cutting. For all his exuberance, Wallace's sporting activities were confined to handball and strapping.

Then Wallace was away: telling the uncomfortable prefect that I was full of myself, invidious, ungrateful, cynical. .... There was no stopping him in these tirades but he must have realized he had overstepped the mark. When the bell to end the session sounded, he detained me. He explained that he had been upset not by my refusal to address the envolopes, because he had made it clear it was a free choice, but by my rank in-gratitude after all he had done for me, the hardening of heart in one he had believed was unspoiled. He said he would talk to my father about me. I was seething but silent. It worried me that he wanted to see my father. I regretted I could not ask Father Curtin to prevent the meeting, as on a previous occasion when he had unwittingly abetted my truancy.

Curtin was the first person I had met who could match my cricket lore. Somewhere in his presbytery packed with cricket books there must have been volumes also on the theology of Test Matches and the spirituality of spin bowling. He spoke of the game with a rueful love as if it were a paradise from which he was excluded; I never found out whether this was due to his clerical state or excess weight.

I had ferreted out arcane cricket manuals in the public library; I knew that cricket books could be consulted free in several secondhand bookshops; I had a collection of Wisdens. Not only had I read C.B. Turner on the art of bowling, I was writing my own study on left-arm leg-spin bowling.

Curtin told me how disappointed he was that, as he had to give lectures in a distant convent, he could not see the New South Wales side, particularly Bill Alley.

I decided to take his place on the first day and give him a report on his return. The match was played at the Carlton Oval. What stuck in my mind was a newcomer with a flowing action who at the end of the day, after opening the bowling, had none for a hundred. Then, with a final flourish, he yorked a tailender. I can still see him completing his follow-through as the ball crashed against the stumps. Lindwall was the name.

Afterwards I had to write a letter, ostensibly from my father, explaining that gastric trouble had kept me from school. I had no more qualms writing it than when I rose from bed, while home with flu or some such ailment, to practice bowling in the backyard once my mother left to do the shopping. My passion for cricket made it a peccadillo which would receive ample absolution from Curtin.

Wallace sat on one of the front desks. "Liam," he asked offhandedly after reading my letter, "how do you spell 'sincerely'?"

"S-i-n-c-e-r-l-y" I answered promptly.

"Good," he said "you've always fancied yourself as another Keats. And how does your father spell it?"

"S-i-n-c-e-r-l-y, sir." Bravely, but my voice was disembodied, "We all spell it that way in our family."

My classmates had not enjoyed themselves so much since Wallace, by his hectoring, last reduced the Jew refugee boy in our class to a confused stammerer.

"I want to ask you father about that Liam," Wallace said, pronoucing my name "Lie-am" and giving me one of his meaningful, above-spectacle-rim looks as when he told a transgressor to stand under the classroom clock, adding, "When the clock strikes, son, I'll remember you."

Curtin had forestalled that meeting and extracted a promise from Wallace that the episode would be forgotten.

But there was no saint who could stop Wallace meeting my father on his return from Sydney, which was why I invoked instant divine justice that

Friday. Although I was too close to foresee it, it is not hard to imagine what happened when my father did meet Wallace.

I had wanted the angel of the Lord to transfix Wallace in mid-accusation. I had wanted the trumpets sounding, as I had dreamt of them, over the Dandenongs for some seconds before it dawned on voluble Wallace that the time for bluff was over.

But Christ was not on call. I should have had more faith in my father who art on earth. Mild-mannered, respectful, he bridled at a Corcoran being bawled out for sticking to his rights. I had briefed him well.

Predictably Wallace, his main attack repulsed, smeared me with what he had promised to forget, my forged note with "sincerly" misspelt.

I realized it only later. My father returned from school in a glow of Corcoran pride obvious as he told us about the confrontation. However he was slightly reserved with me, which I understood only when my younger brother Tim began to play a spelling game.

My father, deep in a murder mystery, asked Tim to spell "sincerely", which he managed.

"You're the only one of us who's not a famous ignoramus, Tim. You've saved the tottering Corcoran reputation. It's even more important," my father continued sweetly, "to be sincere than to know how to spell it."

Touché for both Wallace and myself. I was suffused by anger as well as regret. Had my father claimed to misspell "sincerely" to save my face? I was too ashamed to ask. And furious with Wallace for breaking his promise.

It was a beginning of wisdom. My expectations had been perfervid, but Christ was not around the corner. Instead we have to make do with the Wallaces, the Curtins. I had to recognize that we depart while the world remains. The end will not come with a trumpet blast. Time does its insidious work imperceptibly. It hit me hard the other day when I saw the veins knotted in the back of my wife's hand. It's the heat which does it: I'm sure it's so oppressive because of car fumes. I think of her, of us, as unchanging but those veins showed time is shadowing us, hardening the arteries, silting the heart whose beats — when you reflect on it — are quantifiable and running to their term.

That is why the Witnesses at the door reminded me of that radical hope: that sometime He would come; that Time, stealthy enemy, would not have the very last laugh; that its imperceptible erosion would have a stop. Even some Buddhists will know what I mean.

You Haven't Changed
a Bit

"HERE WE ARE AGAIN, thank goodness."

Matthew Shaw, seated with his parents in the airport departure lounge, turned at the words from Flo, the girl who had sat beside him on the charter flight back to Australia six weeks ago.

"At least you got a good tan out of it," she added, juggling her light luggage as he stood to shake hands, a habit he had acquired in Italy.

"Enjoy yourself in the lackey country?" He harked back to a phrase from the outward flight.

"Not half bad," she admitted, "they've picked up a few wrinkles in the old home town." Matthew imagined that his mother, who was within earshot, would register this with indignation. "To tell the truth though," Flo continued, fishing in her shoulder bag for a cigarette, "can't wait to get back to London — I was terrified I'd break my leg or something and couldn't make the flight."

A broken leg, it occured to Matthew, might have been a good excuse for him to stay longer. He remembered Flo's determination on the outward flight not to be trapped by old ties. On leaving Bahrein, she had read him a letter from a friend who had returned after living in Spain: "Australia's Australia and I could manage without it. To us it looks more like the lackey, than the lucky country.

Everyone claims it's changed but what's unchanged is too much. After Spain, we miss noise, confusion etc. In the suburbs, the silence is suicidal. No one is ever around except our creepy neighbour who gets her kicks from peering through the fence at the baby clothes. Peter and baby and the yellow cat who has cottoned onto us are more interesting than anything I've seen when I've trekked into 'town' — here you have to go to it rather than being part of it. Peter is not saying much, grimly trying to hang on but you remember! — and be warned".

At 30,000 feet over Pakistan it made an impact. The crystalline sameness of the suburbs, the glacial loneliness. Matthew dredged up the phrases but he could not really recapture the feel of Melbourne suburbia. Flo, rather than the letter, revived his apprehension about the six weeks he was to spend in Australia. She was outgoing but there was a plastic quality about her; he suspected she was all surface. The Ashburton she scorned had marked her indelibly. Even her abbeviated name irritated him. He wanted to call her Florence but let it pass. And was irked that, at perhaps 8,000 miles from home, his fastidiousness seemed to be rising like dangerous blood pressure.

It would be hard to pinpoint what had set him at odds with Australia before his departure. Everything and nothing. He told himself his education had fostered expectations which could not be satisfied in Melbourne. But he could not recapture the intense feeling that he had to escape despite his affectionate parents and his friends. He recalled walking past Elizabeth street post office one evening against the crowd streaming to the railway station, repeating to himself that life just had to be different elsewhere.

Sometimes he had a twinge of the same allergy on meeting Australians in Italy. He had written tartly to his friend Gavin Barrymore that the few Australians in Rome prevented nostalgia. Didn't they but, he told himself, closing his eyes and easing back his seat in an attempt to sleep.

Matthew had settled in Rome by chance. He had set out on what was to be a two-year world trip. Teaching in England had led to an English-language school in Rome. The two years had become twelve. With a partner, he had recently established his own school to teach English. After years of worry that his parents might die before he could see them again, he at last had the money for a trip home. He was going for his parents' sake but also to satisfy a curiosity about Australia, about himself.

Matthew barely dozed during the brief darkness but Flo, who had draped a blanket around the distracting legs revealed by a vestigal miniskirt, slept with the abandon of a child, snoring and mumbling. Only thing as intimate as a honeymoon bed, Matthew concluded, was twin seats in a Europe-Australia jet.

Occasionally Matthew cocked an eye at the screen where magnificent men in their flying machines crashed with abandon. When that screen at last faded, dawn seeped along the horizon, a widescreen commercial for creation. I wouldn't care if the plane crashed, was Matthew's last thought before he was awoken by a hostess offering a glass of orange juice.

Strange it's not a sleeping pill, murmured Matthew who recognized the hospital routine designed to prevent rest. He felt he had slept in one of the jet engines. And been spun-dry. Cocky-cage mouth. Golf-ball eyes. Distance is the sickness, he diagnosed, and Australia the cure.

During breakfast, Foghorn resumed transmission. On leaving Rome, Matthew had realized with sinking heart that the passenger directly behind him was an authentic Ocker, solid gristle from ear to ear. But Foghorn had cut out before Beirut, presumably because of beer stupor. Now he was the life of the party again, promising he would play when he hit the big smoke, and reciting his basic philosophical position:

Eat when you're hungry
Drink when you're dry
You can't stuff yourself
with pie in the sky.

The sheer relentless boorishness riled Matthew but he could imagine the paranoic reaction if he told Foghorn to moderate the volume, to put a sock in it. Quailing at the thought of ten thousand pubs across the sunburnt country dominated by such loudmouths, he sought refuge in a copy of the *Bulletin,* puzzling over such names as Bazza McKenzie, Mick Young, Stork, Lionel Murphy, Tony Mundine . . . a foreign country.

Bloated as a battery-fed chicken from constant feeding, Matthew was relieved to descend at Kuala Lumpur airport, only to be stunned by the tarmac's clinging heat.

The frail girls in split skirts, the lackadaisical

moneychanger, the Malaysian signs in the passengers' transit lounge brought home to him that he had broken clear of Rome after more than a decade. He glanced at the displays of pottery and embroidery: modest, decorative, as slight as the perfume-drenched girls at a small cosmetics stand. They barely scratch the surface, thought Matthew, it's too hot to do more, and then cautioned himself against projecting from his own wilted condition. He flopped into an armchair, aimlessly watching other passengers haggle over duty-free goods.

Back in the plane, he found Flo had changed from miniskirt to suede slacks. He objected but she explained her parents would meet her when she landed in Melbourne.

Now his eyes could bear the sunfall over ridges of sandstone cloud. Below, the sea was a purple earth dotted with green lakes. The green was the shallow water ringing myriad atolls. Its light, chemical tone, as exotic as an orchid, made them seem amoeba.

Foghorn still sounded but Matthew screened him out. Flo was determined to tell Matthew about the farewell hambone party her Australian friends had organized in London but now that they were really homing, Matthew's nose was glued to the window.

What stretched below, beneath a Prussian-blue sky which faded to an opaline, heat-hazed horizon, was the arid acne of the continent's interior. The plane was a flying microscope. The thin black lines criss-crossing the surface seemed crazed arteries.

The canvas was creased like a folded map. The reds ranged from clay-brown through ochre to scarlet birthmark patches. It was smudged by purple dye runs. Subtle, abstract but if you were down there, Matthew imagined, it would be pitiless baked mud where you would perish, tongue swelling fit to choke you, while you clawed your way towards the gauzy horizon. Wastes that make man nothing, he mused, Australia is the death of God. Grains of desert sand lodged in his weary eyes.

"Getting off in Sydney, mate? " The steward proferred a disembarcation card.

"No, Melbourne. By this stage, there's not much choice, is there? "

"You can't go wrong," said the steward warmly, "best country in the world."

Don't make me gag on the place while we're still airborne, thought Matthew, momentarily wishing he had returned to Rome from Kuala Lumpur.

The dun-green of eucalyptus became more frequent, the ravines of the Blue Mountains looked formidable despite the plane's altitude, they were banking above Botany Bay. Twelve years accumulating a fare, thought Matthew as the jet slid over Sydney's red tile roofs, then you arrive as easily as if you've taken a local train. Distance telescoped but time was irreversible.

As the plan taxied to a halt, Foghorn announced that Sydney custom officials were invariably a pack of bastards. Matthew warned Flo to tighten her seat-belt further against the cultural shock. It came earlier than expected. Passengers were told there was to be an aerosol spraying before disembarcation. The health officials advanced, their sunraw faces set in a grimace, disinfectant hissing from the cans they held on high.

"Oink, oink," squealed Flo, from beneath the silk scarf she had thrown over her nose, when they had passed. After Sydney, excitement displaced weariness. Although still rather empty, the landscape was at least green.

Tullamarine, almost trafficless, its windows the unreal colour of a nail lacquer: salmon sheen, Matthew named it. The airport was new to him. But his parents were old.

Twelve years had scoured his mother's delicate skin. His father was thinner, almost bald. Matthew, upset, told himself it was only to be expected. But he had not prepared his defences.

"You haven't changed a bit," his mother said when she had blinked away the tears. The words would be echoed throughout his stay, always sounding to Matthew as an appeal to hold time at bay.

"Except for the Pommy accent," said his father, disapproving the change caused by years of Italian vowels, "and the Eye-tie jacket." It was rather an electric blue. "Not to mention the violinist's hair." His father smiled ruefully to soften the blows.

"It's the hair you *used* to have Frank," said Matthew's mother, laughing.

In the cautiously driven Holden, she outlined a packed program for him, including a visit to an aunt he disliked. When Matthew objected that he wanted to find his landlegs, she insisted: "If we don't get things done, it'll be too late at the end."

"Let Matt have a breather Nance," said his father, gripping the wheel as if it were a lifebelt after a shipwreck. "You'll have to make allowances for your mother Matt," he continued as if she were not there, "she's very keyed up."

"Of course you must be tired Matt dear," she

said, then lowered her voice, "your father doesn't hear at all well. I want you to convince him to see a specialist. He'll listen to you Matt, he won't listen to me — not even when he hears me."

Having conveyed the confidential message, she proudly pointed out landmarks as if Matthew were a newcomer. After compact Rome, Melbourne seemed spread thin as pizza.

His father talked about the new football transfer fees and was surprised when Matthew confessed ignorance of the players he mentioned. Matthew sensed he was being treated as if he had been reading Lou Richards in the *Sun* all these years, as if he had never left home, as if he had no other interest than an all-consuming passion for footy. Before Matthew's departure, football-talk had been their lingua franca, a surrogate for more mature or intimate conversation. Matthew was depressed to find his father fall back on it now. He feared he was in for a series of dead encounters, a return to a cemetery.

"Just a cold snack dear," said his mother as the car rolled down the driveway of their Caulfield home, "I was up early to get to the airport and couldn't cook." And hadn't slept for the excitement, Matthew understood, foreseeing that at this rate they would all be emotional wrecks.

When he stepped from the car, he really touched ground. The garden where he had once planted flowers before wanting urgently to escape the ritual of lawnmower and secateurs. The house, the secure realm of his parents, lightfilled, airier than he expected, as if his departure would have plunged it into a grey halflight.

Lunch consisted of broth, cold ham, chicken, mixed salad, pineapple with cream and icecream, lamingtons, fruit cake, lemonade.

"Do you want a ham sandwich dear? " his mother called from the kitchen as he topped off the meal with an apple.

"I'm going to take this ham back," she announced, indignant, "it's like two pounds of cured rubber! "

"Don't," her husband pleaded, but without hope.

"I'm going to," she repeated, "they know me — I won't take second-rate goods."

For some days Matthew woke at 3 a.m., his brain racing, but gradually he adjusted. As his father had now retired from the bank, it was like a long holiday for them all with trips whenever they wanted to the sea or the hills. It was all much happier, easier than he had imagined.

But within a week, he had settled in so well that he locked horns with his father who resented it when Matthew, without thinking twice, criticized Australian attitudes to Europe. In the argument, Matthew felt he was being treated as both foreigner and an inexperienced young man but, as it occured during a visit from friends, both kept their voices low. Like their old arguments, it left Matthew trembling. Affection quickly healed the breach, as both were ashamed by the resurgence of bad blood, but the consequence was that Matthew wanted to see more of his friends, particularly his oldest, Gavin Barrymore.

Golliwog-haired Gavin, who had intended to accompany Matthew to Europe, had married instead and now had seven children. At his

Camberwell home, Gavin had a party for Matthew who unaccountably took a wrong turning on the way. The streets, at dusk, were eerily deserted. Light persisted in the eastern sky as if time had stopped. No telephone boxes where he could ring Gavin for directions, no shops to make enquiries. He felt he could die with the day and no one would notice. The dense life of European cities thinned here, everyone was isolated behind privet hedges. Matthew thought of his mother, who needed human contact like air, marooned in Caulfield when her husband drove to golf or bowls. Eventually he trekked to the main road and found his way to the Barrymore front door before, as he told Gavin wryly, being crazed by solitude.

Time had treated most of his friends kindly; only one, Andy Bisset a surgeon, had aged dramatically: his face was a mask in which only the blue eyes remained recognizable. The others were flourishing, benign: the teachers had manoeuvred themselves into posts where they did not have to teach, the journalists, such as elegant Bruce Hasselton, into positions where they rarely wrote.

Matthew asked after mutual acquaintances but the trails petered out, the questions hung in the air. A voice from the past, he realized, talking about people his friends had not heard of since they last saw him. Matthew was seated on the floor, relaxed, with others gathered around him. Conversation lapsed. Bisset, in his deliberate way, said, "Well Matt, tell us all about it . . ." Suddenly it seemed to Matthew the whole evening had been staged to put him in the arena. He looked around, unsure, wondering if he could open up, trust them. But he

129

was able to parry off Bisset and conversation bubbled back.

Next day he reproved himself. What if Bisset's question had been as innocent as it seemed? And what did it matter anyway, if Bisset had his tongue in his cheek, trying to trap him into inflated spiel about Europe? An opportunity for some good talk if I were not afraid of them judging me, Matthew told himself. Judging me what? Different was the only answer he could give. He felt he was, too, but wondered if it was anything other than twelve more years and the colouring of his Rome surroundings. And asked why, if he wanted his parents to recognize that he had changed, he was wary of his friends noting it. Couldn't he just be himself with both of them? But the self, he now suspected, existed only in the eye of the beholder.

Casual meetings with acquaintances convinced him he was a stranger. Taking his mother to a theatre, he met Noelene Savage, the secretary and parttime actress he used to date. Under a more sophisticated exterior she had closed up and he wondered how it would have gone if she had tried to share with him whatever she was defending. His mother, who liked to believe that dozens of girls had been mad on her son, brought him diligently up-to-date on several of them. Their neighbour Helen Flanders, a plain girl who had an embarrassing crush on him when they were both at secondary school, had become an Anglican nun.

Matthew had lost touch with those who had branched into new activities while those who were doing the same jobs as when he left unaccountably saddened him. Without putting down real roots in

Italy, he reflected, I've become a stranger in my own country, seeing the natives through a distorting glaze of noninvolvement. It had all come to a stop for him twelve years ago.

"I'm a case of arrested development," he told Gavin Barrymore regretfully as a coroner. Gavin did not understand for he imagined the years overseas were all gain; he was still hoping to move to Sydney. But Matthew meant what he said; he had not matured with his mates. He found that, like his father, he had no sense of aging. But the flesh was failing: the backs of his hands showed the first traces of the mottling he had noticed on his father's skin.

As he feared he had forfeited his birthright of involvement, Matthew was unprepared for the impact of Neil Quinn's reappearance. Matthew was leaving the *Era* newspaper office, after calling on Bruce Hasselton, when he felt a tap on his shoulder.

"Aren't you Matt Shaw? "

It took half a second before Matthew recognized Neil Quinn who, for a few years in early secondary school, had been his bosom friend. Because they had the same birthday, they had considered themselves blood brothers.

The sleeves of Neil's spotless white shirt were rolled back to protect the cuffs, the knot of his navy-blue tie was dragged below its unbuttoned collar. He looked a handyman, a trustworthy stakhanovite.

Neil, slightly embarrassed, explained that he was a messenger. Matthew remembered that they were called "messenger boys." In little more than the time it took to walk to the lift with his unchanged, rolling, sailor's gait, Neil told a story of a broken marriage. His two daughters boarded in a country convent. What's it like Matthew kept asking himself, to be a nearly forty-year-old newspaper office messenger when you were a schoolmate of some of the journalists?

"Good on you Matt," said Neil heartily when Matthew, after hearing the sorry tale, outlined his Roman activities. But Neil's attitude, while friendly, had a touch of the deferential. He knows his place, thought Matthew, he knows his place.

"You could do me a good turn," Neil continued, dabbing at his brow with a white, folded handkerchief, "when you get back to the pope's town. Send a postcard to the two kids — here, I'll write you their names and addresses."

Matthew had expected a more onerous request. If only he could do something tangible for others so easily. He asked what he should write.

"Anything — like 'Hope to see you over here some day! ' Will give them a kick." Neil wiped both sides of his left hand over his lips as if cleaning a knife on a plate's edge. "And sign it Uncle Matt."

Matthew could not get out quickly enough. He walked towards Swanston street to catch a tram home, distressed both at the encounter and at his desire to make it brief. Not that Neil had been anything but businesslike, as if he were talking to someone who would have a crowded schedule of appointments.

The city's curlicues of commercial Gothic seemed more than ever hoary marzipan as Matthew recalled their friendship. For some time they had felt as unified as Siamese twins even though he had found Neil's slummy Richmond house a surprising contrast to his own comfortable home. But then Matthew, discovering he was intellectually superior, had begun humiliating Neil.

He stood at his tramstop. Already, although it was not yet 7 p.m., the city was drained of life. Matthew felt the straight streets were somehow to blame. What remained were clashing shop signs, discordant buildings, a utilitarian eyesore. As he recognized the ugliness, he knew exactly how it had been with Neil. Like an acid eating through veneer, the awareness bit through the blandness of his sojourn.

With classmates, they were crossing Elsternwick park to the dressing rooms before a football match. Neil rolled along, dogged and amiable, gripping his oversize Gladstone bag, his cap set like a helmet on his squarish head, on his brilliantined, blonde, brushed-back hair. Even then Neil had seemed bent by hard yakka. Matthew had cut him to ribbons by remarks which set their friends laughing. As usual, Neil had not reacted but, tongue-tied, gradually lagged behind. Matthew had encouraged his target to keep pace but, when he dropped away, Matthew was pleased to be left with brighter boys.

Their friendship subsided rather than soured. Neil did not nuture resentment while Matthew, once his supercilious attitude had established his superiority, was prepared to be condescending.

It reminded Matthew of the fly torture with which some classmates had combated boredom. Some merely caught flies and released them, by raising the fingers of their clenched fist, after announcing departure of the next fly flight. Others detached their wings one at a time, watching for signs of suffering. The scientific spirit. Nellie Blighs.

He had adopted a comparable attitude to Neil. He had been convinced that deep down, in some secret vault of the heart, the relationship was unchanged. All that was expressed, however, were shrivelling words as he tried to goad Neil to react. And they called Asians inscrutable, he reflected, which brought to mind the Chinese burns his classmates used to inflict on one another. Just testing. The wrist twisted until it scorched. A slow burn, that was what he had applied to their relationship. Was Neil's patience complicity? Matthew recalled reading that there is always complicity between torturer and tortured, whose roles are assigned by fate.

On leaving school, they had lost touch. He had heard Neil was making money driving his own taxi. It had seemed appropriate that Neil should be a moneymaker while he himself, as a teacher, looked like earning little. But now he did not take easily to the thought that while he and his friends were comfortable, Neil should be a "messenger boy" who knew his place.

Overseas, memory had been his great consolation. Memory, Matthew had come to believe, was mystical. It arrived as unexpected and swift as a swallow, delivering whole scenes or incidents intact. There was another memory also, more vague and constant, which assured him he possessed his past. Since his return, he had discovered how unreliable it was. Walking along the streets of his boyhood in Windsor he found they were different from his memory of them. Not only were they wider or narrower, they had a quotidianity whereas his memory somehow pictured them as more dramatic. He had made the same discovery with his parents' house: what he carried with him was a shrunken version of what it was, shrunken but with the colours deepened. Now he had found that his memory conveniently rewrote his own past, ignoring his instinctive cruelty like an official Soviet history. He wondered what sort of an insufferable young prig he had been.

In a tin trunk under the house he found a diary written, three years after the break from Neil, when he was sixteen. He barely remembered the details recorded and did not at all recognize the diarist.

His reading included Lloyd C. Douglas's *Forgive Us Our Trespasses,* Francis Gerard's *Wotan's Wedge,* Maurice Walsh's *Road to Nowhere,* Richard Dehan's *That Which Hath Wings,* Galsworthy's plays and Noel Coward's *Middle East Diary.* He liked them all but did not rate highly Miles Franklin's *Old Blastus of Bandicoot* nor Shaw's *Arms and the Man.* The films he ingested included *Music for Millions, Road to Utopia, A Song to Remember, The Suspect* and *The Song of Bernadette.* He enjoyed the radio program "Hullo the Hospitals" and Tommy Trinder's humour. He wanted to be an agricultural scientist. With his father, he built a deck chair and made a putting green in the back yard.

How, Matthew asked, could that student who was about to begin studying for the Leaving examination and called his diary "Ego I," believe he was anyone's intellectual superior? He must have been more sympathetic, Matthew concluded, at the much earlier stage when he followed David and

Dawn into fairy land to the sound of Ponchielli and, encouraged by Nicky and Nancy Lee's radio tips, hunted for chocolate frogs all over the house.

Matthew also dug out a notebook from his first university year in which his family was likewise subject to the ukase of his superiority. Once again he could barely see himself in the notemaker. We become a different person, he told himself, every three years or so. He hoped he had changed a lot but there was continuity, he had to admit, in the cutting down of Neil and his family to less than life size.

He was as indignant against his younger self as against what had been done by others to Neil. It was indignation I used to feel, he recognized, not merely fastidiousness, the indignation which derives from involvement. He had been intent on remaking his parents, on remaking Australia, that was it. In Italy, by contrast, the problems were not his. It was less wearing.

The whiff of that burning indignation was like the smell of cordite to an old soldier. He had not changed entirely, thank God. Merely encrusted. He had been something other than a cruel thirteen and a priggish sixteen. Even though the crusading spirit had been all of a piece with his intolerance, his scathing criticism of his parents and much else, he was consoled that his reaction to Neil Quinn showed something of it survived. Not that it had achieved anything: instead of remaking Australia, he had left it. Life seemed to have disposed of him nonchalantly although with kid gloves.

It had been harsher with Neil Quinn. Matthew sought him but found he was on leave. He asked himself what he would have said or done anyway?

Too much separated them now, he had been glad to escape Neil's company. Demythologize the equality legend which consoled Neil? Act the superior intellect again after quarter of a century? Oh chuck it Shaw, he admonished himself.

Nevertheless he rang the boarding school whose address Neil had given him. After a voice had croaked "Mr Neil Quinn? " twice there was a long pause. Matthew presumed a decrepit nun had gone to seek Neil for surely he would be with his daughters. Then a young voice said: "Hullo Daddy."

"I'm not your Daddy." Matthew vainly tried to recall the girl's name, "I'm your uncle Matt." He wondered if his mother was listening from her bedroom.

"Uncle Matt?"

Was her tone incredulous or hostile? Matthew was uncertain whether he was supposed to be a brother of Neil or of his wife.

"Most of the time I live in Rome."

He could hear her heavy breathing. Asthma? Or merely because she had run to the phone?

"In Italy," he continued, although there was no encouragement, "long way away. I'm passing through — just wanted to say hullo to you."

Was he imagining bad vibes through the earpiece?

"Give my best wishes to your sister too, will you darling."

He was uncertain about the "darling". Despite himself, he began to feel antipathy for the girl.

"I've never heard of any uncle Matt." Stubborn.

How old was she? He saw a freckled face, pugnacious.

"You'd have known me, though, if I was living here all the time. I'd come to take you out."

"The nuns told us not to take any notice of strange men."

She would scream blue murder at the slightest provocation. Morals charge — filthy habits picked up in Italy.

"Don't worry: I'm ringing from Melbourne. Safe distance." For both of us.

"Why'd you say you was my dad? "

"I didn't, it's all a misunderstanding."

"Yair — I believe Sister Lawrence."

How could a sister be called Lawrence? He tried to recall a female saint Lawrence but got no further than Lawrence of Arabia.

"Ask your dad about me."

"Yair, I'm gunna."

"Must go now, darling. Have to catch my plane. All the best to you both. I'll be thinking about you."

Head in flames, he rang again, hissing at the nun not to repeat her mistake, that he was not Neil Quinn but merely wanted to know if he was visiting his daughters.

"He only comes every so often."

Sharply, he asked how many times a year.

"Only a few times — but he's so hard worked. Who are you to be asking? "

"A relative."

"The girls need visitors."

"Yes, but I'm just passing through — from Rome."

"It's Father Quinn, is it? " she asked, deferential

138

now, "I didn't realize. It must be wonderful being in Rome."

"No place is quite like your own though, Sister. I want you to let the Quinn girls out and about a bit. They won't be living all their life in a convent, if you know what I mean. I must catch my plane now Sister — keep the faith."

When Matthew farewelled Gavin, he heard a story about Quinn: one night, while a taxi driver, Quinn had picked up an elegantly dressed man. When he turned to collect his fare, he saw it was Erwin Rosen who had been a German Jewish refugee classmate and the butt of all jokes. Neil, in his rough-and-ready way, had expressed his pleasure. Rosen had grunted a few times and, at the end, corrected the driver. "Not Erwin," he said, "but Doctor Rosen." With that he had left, giving an insultingly large tip.

Matthew could understand Rosen, after stopping classmates' shit for years, spreading some of his own. But the story increased his distress over Neil, still coming up smiling with an unshakeable belief that Australia meant mateship when brains and environment ruthlessly classified people.

That evening, when Matthew kissed his mother goodnight as she dozed at the television, she mentioned Neil Quinn. "His mother worked at Rosella's no less, poor soul. I'd heard Neil was driving a taxi — was always hoping to find him at the wheel when I took one."

If she had found him, Matthew was sure, her gregariousness would have ousted her snobbery. With her usual relish, she told her husband about the meeting. He did not remember Neil Quinn but, true to the equality ethos, maintained there was nothing wrong with being a messenger.

"But he's no boy," his wife pointed out, "he's exactly the same age as Matthew."

"Any job is worth doing well," he said, slapping the newspaper he was folding as if annoyed at the interruption.

"You don't hear, Frank. He's messenger for chaps who were his classmates — like that Bruce Hasselton who lives on the other side of the park," his wife answered, conveying the full indignity of the situation. "How'd you like Matthew to be doing that?"

No answer, but it must have occured to them both that at least they would not have to wait twelve years to see their son.

Towards the end of his stay, Matthew realized his mother's impetuosity, his father's obstinacy still exasperated him. But he became increasingly worried by the possibility that he might not see them again. It was their departure which would be definitive, rather than his own. Sitting in the back garden after dinner, when he mentioned that he might not have the fare to fly out, even if they were seriously ill, his father told him not to worry.

"It's strange," Matthew ventured, "it's so right sitting here with you both but it seems so impossible when I'm in Rome."

His father, reclining in a deck chair, sat up. He wasn't at all sure what his son meant.

"When you're in Rome, it's hard to imagine being here," Matthew elaborated, "and when you're here, Rome seems unreal. But I'm at home in both places."

Matthew wasn't sure what he meant either. He guessed he wanted imagination to be the real thing, to be with his parents and to be in Rome at the same time, longing for a communion that was not of this world. Could his parents follow him? He could not throw them a line. They talked in low tones until late. Inconsequential talk but they had learnt to take feelings on trust.

Matthew managed to ring his journalist friend Hasselton, who had been on an assignment in the Northern Territory, on the morning he was to depart. He told him had been upset to see his former classmate running around as a messenger boy. Easygoing Hasselton was unmoved.

"Don't sweat too hard over that one — Neil has other resources."

Matthew asked what he meant.

"He makes a few bob on the side," was the enigmatic answer, "wouldn't lose any sleep because of him."

Had his bleeding heart bled unnecessarily?

"Don't talk in riddles man, come clean."

"Can't talk too easily here Matt," said Hasselton, "and it's not too cut-and-dried anyway. I'll tell you the complicated story when I see you."

"Thanks," said Matthew, "but that's not much help. I'll have to wait until you score an inaugural to Rome — I'm on my way to Tullamarine."

He could have counted on anyone else to write but Hasselton's letters were as rare and brief as poor men's telegrams. Matthew always wondered how he managed to put an article together.

On the way to the airport with his parents, Matthew promised that he would be back in three years although he had no idea how to manage it. The chill of those three long years struck them all but at least it was something to grasp.

In three years would he still find Neil Quinn a messenger boy, he asked himself. Or, more to the point, would he look for him? Departure aborted his concern. He feared his links with Australia were becoming as tenuous as a jet trail. At least his mother had agreed to bake cakes and send them to the Quinn girls. Her slapdash makeup indicated how flustered she was.

"Do you like my hat dear? " she asked, even though she had already worn it several times on outings with him. The previous day she had quizzed him on what it was like to fly in a jet.

The drive to the airport was brutally short and the wait in the departure lounge, which opposed a white plastic surface to sentiment, agonizingly long.

"Couldn't you squeeze me into your case? " his mother asked, for her husband claimed he could not afford to send her to Rome. But there was no room: without her husband's knowledge, she had packed it tight with jars of Vegemite; fruit cake with icing; several of his father's singlets, shirts and socks; family photographs and heirlooms.

Awareness of this loot had inhibited Matthew when, at the last minute, his father asked him if he wanted to take one of his overcoats, which Matthew had admired, to Rome. Matthew had left to his father a favourite yellow voile shirt. They wore the same size, although the collar was ample for his father whose neck was shrinking.

Matthew needed a coat but, after a moment's hesitation, declined the offer. He seemed to have ripped everything from his parents. He did not want to take advantage of their affection to plunder further. Besides, he knew that his father, like himself, was cautious with possessions and could only be generous by intent. His mother, a contrast in this as in almost everything else, was instinctively generous, disposing as freely of emotions and of other's possessions as of her own.

Conversation in the departure lounge was fitful. They tried to keep it light and cheery and, to Matthew's surprise, his father told a fresh story about a dangerous wartime flight. His mother went to a corner to cry but regained control. From her bag, she dragged a black satin eyeband hastily sewn to an elastic head piece: "So you'll sleep over China."

"I don't want to look like bloody Mandrake." Matthew, grinning, held it high on two spread fingers as if it were a shanghai.

"Take it," said his father quietly, "it'll give your mother pleasure."

"Oh no," she said quickly, hearing as sharply as ever, "if he doesn't want it, I'll wear it while you're driving."

"I'll take it," said Matthew, using it as a pretext to give his mother a kiss, "frighten the wits out of the other passengers — not that they have too many," he added as Foghorn came to mind.

Then they fell silent for aching moments until he heard Flo, the Australia he would have beside him all the way to Rome, her "Here we are again, thank goodness".

Beirut the Baleful

ALTHOUGH MORTON had not expected the telephone to crash to the floor, he was exhilarated by the bakelite breaking and shoved the typewriter after it, catching a glimpse of Atallah gawking as he lunged next at the cash register.

The cashier had provoked his rage by offering Lebanese change for his $20 bill. "Mickey Mouse money," Morton had shouted to climax the discussion as he started turning over the cashier's office equipment.

Others in the queue restrained him and the cashier, trembling, took his name so that the management could dock his pay for the damages. Morton carried his dinner tray to a far table to eat by himself. He recognized that he had taken too many farewell drinks with his few office friends but he felt fine after his outburst. After all, he had said clearly he wanted only American change. Piastres would be useless to him tomorrow. Who needed them?

He said as much to Atallah who was clearing the tables. The sight of Atallah had probably aggravated his anger, Morton reflected. He wanted to show Atallah that he could shake the dust of Beirut off his boots.

"Never seen you so angry Mr Morton, sir." Atallah had stopped at his table.

Morton explained that, as he was leaving for London tomorrow, piastres were useless. It sound petty even to him."So you won't have to pay for the damage!" said Atallah quickly, sitting with a cloth in the hand propped under his chin.

As usual, Atallah managed to make Morton uneasy. First by identifying immediately why he was carefree despite the damage he had done. And second by not knowing his place, by sitting at the table he was supposed to be clearing. You never knew where you were with him: one minute he was using the exaggerated "Mr Morton, sir"; the next he was pushing his askew face against yours.

Morton had first met Atallah as a fellow employee. The Americans had employed Atallah as office boy because of his good English and knowledge of Beirut. Morton suspected that he himself had been taken on as a kind of Super Atallah for his Syrian visa, which was denied to the Americans.

Atallah had not lasted. Morton did not know if it was because he was too dumb or too clever. Sometimes he seemed one, sometimes the other, making it difficult to say whether tragic circumstances had retarded his intelligence or sharpened it. This air of patient suffering approached the subversive in an office where even the decor had to be optimistic. A strike in his favour was that he was some sort of Christian. But then word spread that, although it had been presumed he was a local, he was Palestinian and possibly a Fedayeen sympathizer. The imponderables were too many for an office were there was a running joke about Al Fatah speaking with a Cicero, Chicago, accent. Atallah had been dismissed and no Arab replacement hired.

However, Atallah had still managed to find Morton to request favours. It unnerved Morton that Atallah seemed to know his every movement. Atallah wanted his assistance to migrate to Australia. Morton told him bluntly that Australia was not in the market for albino Arabs. Once, in the "Aussie" seafront bar, Atallah had offered Morton a handful of gold coins if he arranged for his migration. Morton would gladly have given Atallah gold coins to be freed of the feeling that each time he turned a corner he might find the Arab loitering nearby.

Finally, in a coffee bar, Atallah had produced a pistol saying he would use it if Morton did not arrange his departure from Lebanon promptly. Morton talked Atallah out of his homicidal mood without revealing his manic fear he would be killed casually by such a puny idiot. Eventually Atallah pocketed the pistol as if it were a toy. Morton, recovering quickly, called him The Wild Colonial Boy and taught him the lines:

> ... He waved his little toy
> I'll fight but not surrender
> cried the wild colonial boy.

But he hated those long seconds Atallah had held his pistol at the ready. For Morton, Atallah's gesture expressed Beirut's casual violence which he had only recently recognized. The city had soured and he was glad to be shrugging it off. He would have been glad, he believed, even if the Yanks had not told him he had come to the end of the road — the

146

Damascus road. They now had other channels of contact with the Syrian capital.

As Morton had not seen Atallah for months, he had been surprised to find him in the American company's canteen.

"Penn know you're working here?"

It was a potential threat to offset Atallah's know-ledge that Morton would evade paying the damage he had done.

"Not yet," was Atallah's answer. Penn and others from central office rarely ate in the canteen: for them it would be a kind of slumming. Morton would not be there himself unless his office mates had left Beirut for the weekend.

"You want to keep it that way," Morton said, "and keep you nose clean here too."

Morton tipped his head in the direction of the boss waiter and Atallah resumed his work, although with a hangdog air when the convention demanded a smiling enthusiasm.

Morton wondered idly at Atallah's descent from office boy to waiter and his return to work for the same Americans who had treated him as a Sambo. Damned if they'd have me eating their shit again, Morton told himself, putting Atallah out of mind and asking what he would do from tomorrow. He was wary of returning directly to Sydney after so many years. If he could stand the climate, he would size up prospects in London.

He walked to the counter to order fruit salad with icecream. The barboy requested payment but, anger flaring again, Morton said he had already paid the cashier. The boy objected that the cashier had been closed for an hour. Morton baulked, asking himself where the hour had gone. He shouted that he was not paying twice and the chief waiter, who had seen his squabble with the cashier, told the boy to give him the salad and icecream. Morton ate it at the counter, staring down those looking at him. Use a long spoon, he reminded himself, when supping with wogs, wops and boongs.

He left for the YMCA where he had shifted for his last days in Beirut. He passed the "Aussie" bar whose proprietors gave him preferential treatment out of deference to blurred wartime memories. As he did not want to tell them of his departure, he ignored it. A moon-streak silvered the black sea. Never runs a decent surf, thought Morton who felt he would have cut a broad swathe if only he could have performed there on a surfboard. But then the Mediterranean was tame, a puddle suitable only for nabobs pirouetting in motorboats beyond the St George hotel. More a swamped service station, he liked to say, than a sea.

At the beginning, he had made sallies into the glittering world oiled by desert shieks who came to Beirut to play and by the trading talents of the Phoenicians' heirs. But after he found he could not keep the pace, he had recognized what lay behind the facade. Literally behind the facade because only a few streets behind the luxury hotels lining the sea-front the poverty was as black, rheumy, lurid as anything he had seen when the ship which brought him to Europe twelve years ago, in 1960, had opened his eyes to the running sores called Bombay, Aden and Port Said.

All day, whole families tried to sell the same food or the same useless objects as swarms of others.

Their lean-tos were constructed with refuse. The craxy quilt of brand names, Texaco, Campbell's, Unilever, could have been proleterian pop. The senseless collage suggested the inhabitants were flotsam in a flood of waste, debris among debris, with something of the pointless indestructibility of plastic bags. They were mute, too beaten to be any threat to the passerby but nevertheless disquieting. Morton understood more than he cared to acknowledge. He had closed his mind against certain perceptions while walking frequently through streets which reinforced his maturing decison to leave Beirut. He would not be one of the targets, he promised himself, when they came screaming out of the slums with their scimitars slashing. He suspected it would never happen, that it was only wishful thinking on his part.

He threw himself on the bed in his room whose walls were cocoa-coloured. The earsplitting jets, which had ruined his sleep since he moved to the YMCA, now presaged his depature. In a few hours, he thought, I'll be sitting pretty cracking *their* eardrums. And then he realized that he had left his ticket and passport in the office. The canteen scene had put them out of mind.

Reluctantly he rose. Early shuteye would have been appropriate for a purposely low-toned last evening. As he did not know when he would be earning again, he walked to the office rather than take a taxi.

It seemed that, for once, he surprised Atallah who leant against a doorway some distance from the office, a folded satchel under his arm and, although it was a mild night, hunched as if against cold.

149

"Just thinking of you Mr Morton," he said delighted.

"Odd occupation."

"No," said Atallah oblivious of Morton's dry tone, "only one in there ever treat me decently."

"We were both their niggers, Atallah," Morton said with fellow feeling, "linked by our leg chains."

Atallah took Morton's arm warmly and they stolled toward the office. Morton, wanting above all to protect the dollars in this jacket's inside pocket, wondered what to do if Atallah pulled the pistol on him again. If he has it, Morton reasoned, it must be in his far pocket.

Morton was thankful that Atallah had not taken his hand as was the local custom.

"You're one we can count on for help," said Atallah, as if offering a privileged invitation. Morton, slowing, said not to count on him but Atallah insisted that Morton could help in his people's struggle for justice.

From his satchel, he extracted a wad of cyclostyled sheets. He thrust them at Morton, asking him to leave them in the office. Morton riffled through them: heated denunciations of American imperialism accompanied by demands for justice and threats of vengeance. Morton, however, was preoccupied with the thought that somehow Atallah had known he was to go to the office. But it was impossible, for half an hour ago he had not even known himself.

Morton sensed Atallah was the bearer of all the bottled-up misery he had to escape. He dropped the sheets, kicking the bundle resoundingly before it touched ground. Atallah watched the sheets swirl groundwards without attempting to gather them. We'll see if he's interested in the freedom struggle or my money, thought Morton as exhilarated as when he had tipped over the cashier's equipment.

"Why did you go to talk with our students?" was all Atallah said. But Morton could not tell him. Perhaps attracted by the explosive cocktail of an American-subsidized university and Palestinians getting their kicks out of loathing Americans. Perhaps because the American university in Beirut gave him the feeling that he could link up with his Sydney University years. Evidently the mistaken word that he was a sympathizer had reached Atallah but the lesson Morton had drawn was that the university was not his scene.

"I must have been slumming," said Morton with a taunting smile.

"Passing on what you heard to Penn?"

"No, kept clear of that." They had not tried to use him that way.

"We're all dragged into it," Atallah said. "You're lucky to get out. For us, it's one big prison."

"Not my country," said Morton, refraining from adding "thank Allah."

Atallah pleaded for Morton, from London, to help him leave Lebanon. But Morton hoped Beirut and its problems would dissolve behind him like the tailstream of the jet. Atallah was as persistent as ever. Morton scanned the street for help but there was only a bent men on the other footpath, wheeling a bicycle past a large 7-UP sign.

If he pulls his stupid pistol on me now, thought Morton, I could be leaving tomorrow in a hearse. He could do nothing for Atallah: he saw him as fated to remain in Beirut with only his half-sly, half-stupid wits to cope with its fermenting frustrations. But he told Atallah what he wanted to hear, that he would contact him from London.

Atallah smiled lopsidedly, saying Morton was a real friend and requesting one last favour: that he bring some sheets of Mr Penn's writing paper from the office.

"Why the hell should I?" asked Morton, truculent again, sensing there was no end to Atallah's needs.

"Because you show yourself a true friend," said Atallah passionately, "you want to leave Lebanon like that I know."

"Bit of robbery to prove I'm one of the boys," said Morton lightly, "you know Penn locks his room every night."

Atallah, confounding Morton once again, said Miss Harrison kept a supply of Penn's paper.

"I'm not promising anything," said Morton, turning into the office building.

His airline ticket with passport lay in the drawer where he had left them. He had not wanted to see again the office with its trim desks, the typewriters which he would have liked to tip over, the bright, non-figurative paintings, and photographs of desert oil fields. Moving cautiously, as if under observation, he drifted into Miss Harrison's cubicle. A box of tissues, an inhaler, a stack of *Time* and *U.S. News and World Report,* a framed photograph of a bucktoothed boy on a horse were the spoor marks of the vinegary old virgin who revelled in Penn's reflected power. Morton recalled her emu-bright eye on him whenever he relaxed and her question:

"Ever worked with Americans before Mr Morton?"

It would only take a call to the police, he thought, to denounce the Fedayeen black-mailer loitering below. But with hysteria running high, he did not know how that would pan out. Keep you nose clean, he counselled himself.

More effective would be a note to Mr. Penn, or better go right to the top, stringy Miss Harrison herself. An Arab aims to rape you. Remember Atallah who was sacked for sufficient reasons? He has insinuated himself into the canteen. Ground class in the couscous? Strychnine in the sherbert? Can this state of affairs continue? Your country needs you! See to it.

He took a sheet of paper to write a provocative farewell note but thought better of it. His fingers responded to the sheet's texture. He held it against the light the read the imprint HAMMERMILL BOND Made in U.S.A. Quilty surface, palest yellow which against the light revealed swirls of white like chicken down. Discreetly, below the company's name: Robert R. Penn.

He longed for a Hammermill Bond life: airconditioned office with wall-to-wall carpets, leatherfaced desk equipment, a servile secretary, a yacht moored at the St. George, tennis twice weekly, not a worry in the world and an ability to shove shit sandwiches down the throat of anyone on the staff.

Initially, Morton had believed he was to be accepted as an almost-American. The world was for winners, he had learnt in Beirut, and he wanted to be one. But he was gradually made to understand that non-American locally-employed staff lived in a no-man's land between the lords of creation and the wogs.

He took a sheaf of the Robert R. Penn writing paper, believing it would divert Atallah from his dollars. If Atallah created mischief for Penn, it would be the least of Morton's worries. He took some sheets for himself also. They would come in handy in the loo the following morning. Let Penn be on the receiving end of crap from him for once.

Atallah was standing opposite the entrance. A sitting target, Morton thought, if he had summonded the riot squad. Nice guys finish last, one of Penn's saws, came to mind when he gave the paper to Atallah as if he, Morton, were his greatest benefactor. Free finally of Atallah, he decided to walk along the seafront rather than return directly to the YMCA.

Buoyant now, he found the touts' invitations flattering rather than irritating. Near the St George he stood studying the posters for the casino. As he had burnt his fingers there early on, it was easy to avoid the temptation to make a big kill on his last night.

He strolled instead to a night club where he had once known one of the strippers, a local who used a French name. She had left for America. He ordered a scotch on the rocks which he would nurse for the whole performance. Despite a desire to enjoy himself, he found the strippers unstimulating. They now used an energetic American bump-and-grind style instead of Parisian rhythmic teasing. Yanks loused even this, he told himself. Still worse was the nightmarish, psychedelic staging used with a self-absorbed blonde billed as Frankfurt Fanny. Two

pasty English lesbians explored each other
disdainfully. The audience was excited by their act
but for Morton it evoked crummy London, walk-up
apartments with dominant prostitutes, cold flesh,
specks of dust in the milk.

By contrast, the eruptive rhythms of a young
Turkish belly-dancer excited him and he set his
mind on having her later, cost what it might.
Something to remember in London. But the longer
he thought about it, the more cautious he became.
Not only because she would be costly but he feared
all his money might be stolen if he went with her.
Getting out intact was the main thing, he reminded
himself, London ran to Turks as well as lesbians.
Instead he bought a souvenir bottle of arak and,
grasping it tightly, set out for the YMCA.

Along the sea-promenade, a handsome youth
offered to take him to young virgins in a nearby flat.
Morton asked if the youth's mother or sister were
available.

"A Turkish girl", said the boy, " all shaven, she is
waiting just for you." I'll bet, though Morton, with
the keepers of the harem ready to cut off my balls
and take my money. He had braved that temptation
in the nightclub. The boy followed him, begging for
his custom.

Morton asked if this was the only work he could
find. "I'm student," the boy pleaded, "but I must
eat too. You like to try Armenian girl, only
fourteen?"

His eyebrows met over deerlike eyes. He had the
deferent charm, the vulnerability Morton had
found everywhere when he first came to Beirut. He
was no threat, no threat at all. Surprising himself,

Morton drew out a $20 bill for the boy, but quickly changed it for a $10 one. The boy thanked Morton guardedly as if expecting he might all of a sudden claim it again.

His rare magnanimity cheered Morton as he sauntered the promenade indifferent to other touts. He felt he had settled his debts with Beirut, that he was free to loathe it and leave it. He wondered how he had once ignored the tremors of violence he now sensed at every step. Beirut the beautiful was a pretty postcard which at any moment could be stained with real blood.

When he entered the YMCA, the waiting police politely asked him to empty his pockets. He immediately thought of the Robert R. Penn paper he carried with his dollars in his inside pocket. He began with his outside pockets. To his surprise he pulled out a folded sheet with a numbered diagram. Thick paper with a waterproof, military air to it, he noted. If people were paper, it occurred to him incongruously, he would assess them more swiftly. The police quickly read it as a key to the Fedayeen camps with information on their strength.

He wondered whether Atallah had slipped it into his pocket before or after he had jettisoned the cyclostyled sheets. Probably before, he decided, because Atallah had been so calm he must have known he was in his power.

He showed the officials his passport stamped "Australian citizen and British subject" which, for the first time, struck him as suspiciously ambiguous. Without knowing why, he said he was represented by the British consul. "We find most agents are," said the older official, pulling at his moustache as if he had dared greatly.

Usually Morton considered Lebanese officials a laugh but now he found their presence concentrated the mind wonderfully. He knew the diagram, by itself, would not prove much if whoever had ordered his detention still required proofs. But, together with a letter on Penn's personal paper, it could damn him sufficiently to reassure people that foreign devils were being trapped.

He wished he had violent, machine-gun rapid Arabic to curse Atallah and Beirut. His mistake, he saw starkly, was not to have left once he penetrated the facade. He recognized that he had become half-clever, half-stupid like Atallah but without the Arab's skill in survival. It flashed on him that Atallah's face recalled photographs of pilots with features distorted under pressure.

Beirut the baleful was to blame: Morton had sensed that it demanded victims. Curiosity killed this cat he thought despondently, feeling it was fate and that he had been born with defeat in his bones. As they led him away, he asked for his bottle of arak. It was handed to him: as he was doing something for the country, he deserved its consolations.

Cameraman

TO UNDERSTAND how it was, you need to know that at school we were occasionally illuminated by bolts from the cloud of unknowing such as that hurled by a zealous layman who one day addressed our class of fifteen-year-olds. He told us we should prefer marrying a Catholic Hottentot to a beautiful non-Catholic neighbour.

For years we had been responding to missionary appeals to "buy a black baby in Africa" without realizing that we might have been anticipating a bride price. However, none of us set sail for Africa to test the zealot's words.

It was the ideal which was important. But the narrowness which went with it could be stifling. I recalled the startling suggestion only years later when my elder sister Moira took logic to a paradoxical conclusion.

That day, in which fog had been dispersed by sun, began placidly with my mother and me reading the Sunday papers in the lounge. I had been to 9 o'clock Mass, my mother was no longer able to go and we presumed Frank, Moira's son who was staying with us briefly, was at 10 o'clock Mass.

The peace was broken by the clap of a book falling in Frank's room. When my mother had called him twice Frank finally appeared, thin and sleepy, head, as always, lowered diffidently, face scarred by acne.

"Thought you were at Mass Frank, my boy," she said, coming straight to the point. By now there was barely time for him to arrive at 11 o'clock Mass before the angels which, we used to be told, assisted at the altar and were upset by latecomers.

"Do I have to go?" Uncertain because he was an acne-anguished adolescent in his grandmother's house but you could not miss the glint of steel.

"Don't you know Catholics go to Mass on Sunday, Frank?" My mother's voice quavered but it would have been a mistake to take it as a sign of weakness. At times she was not merely firm but harsh.

"Most of them go just as an insurance policy against hell." Even though he was long and lank, his lowered head gave the impression he was looking upwards. He barely opened his mouth.

"Fear of the Lord," said my mother, " is the beginning of wisdom. Your mother might raise you like a heathen but, while you're in my house, you'll please observe the Sunday obligation."

Frank's lips pleated in one corner but it was more likely he was throttling a retort than tears. Off he went, presumably to Mass, with a dispirited bend to his shoulders.

It was a toll exacted from my mother as well. She had paid heavily when I left the seminary. I was born nine months after my mother prayed for a son, vowing she would return him to the Lord as a priest. Following Moira's birth, she had suffered two miscarriages. I graduated from altar boy through sodalities to the seminary but found it was not for me even though I could not convince mother of that.

Now I was more or less companion-nurse for her, a job Moira should have undertaken but she was always on her independence kick. At least it gave me a base while waiting for opportunities in movie making.

I wandered into Frank's room after he left for Mass. I expected him to be deep into *Mr. Midshipman Easy* or *Captains Courageous,* as I had been at his age, but instead Trotsky's *History of the Russian Revolution* lay open on his bed and Marx's works were stacked beside it.

Admittedly curiosity took me there but if it had not been for a phone call from Moira, I would have cooled off by leaving the house altogether. Moira had rung to tell me she was on her way and made me promise I would be at home when she arrived.

My mother's vigilante activities had been exercised ruthlessly in respect to Moira although with scarce results.

"Is he baptized?" she had asked when Moira had announced she would marry Franz, the milkman who became Frank's father.

Franz was Lutheran if one went far enough back but, in theory at least, my mother would have preferred a Catholic Hottentot. Franz was more accepted in the neighbourhood than his father who was known, until his dying day, as a German Herman. Bigger-boned than most of the locals, Franz had a particularly flaxen fairness. "Squarehead" was occasionally used for him but suspicion was mitigated by the fact that he was a strong swimmer and, on his day, an irresistible tennis player.

Within the family, all Twomey children were regarded as geniuses but even outsiders recognized that Moira was bright and forceful. She was a highly quoted secretary with an unfortunate penchant for bringing home stray cats and dogs. Mother placed Franz in this category. For her the match was a catastrophe as total as anything in Greek drama. Her brilliant daughter with a heathen milkman of German stock! That he was beyond the religous pale was a blasphemy. That he was German was far worse than the skeleton in my mother's cupboard: her grandmother had been English but never a word was breathed about this dilution of Irish stock. To cap it all, a milkman when the Twomeys were white-collar people. Grandfather had worked in a bicycle factory but my father had been a clerk in government service. Throwing herself at a milkman! Unheard of; anyone would think the girl could not leave home quickly enough.

Franz, of course, had to take instruction from young Father Mangin who was effervescent with Vatican Council ideas years before it took place and was one of the first of our priests to be laicized when it had. Mangin was enthusiastic about instructing Franz but made no headway.

"Poor soil for seeding," my mother observed to all and sundry, except Moira. Truth was, we only knew how to implant two strains of Catholicism: Irish and Italish. We did not know how to tend the German species.

At that time my mother was our parish altar society but she would have liked the marriage ceremony to take place without a congregation in an unadorned church. As it was, on account of our relatives' inability to coordinate their activities as well as embarrassment over the match, few attended.

However, joviality prevailed at the wedding breakfast. Only my mother was dismayed by what she considered the morganatic aspect of the marriage. Her expression suggested that offspring of the deplorable union which were not still-born would be crippled.

In fact, they had bonny babies: Frank, as rotund and outgoing as he had now become thin and introverted, and Gretel, five years younger, who was my mother's pet once she recovered from the shock of the name.

My mother, who was fierce in her affections, could not maintain her disapproval of the marriage against such evidence. Her only plaint was that, after twelve yars, there were not more children. But not even she was capable of a direct confrontation on this point with Moira who, most of the time, was more than a match for her.

Then Franz, so stoutly timbered that he seemed unsinkable, sickened and died within a matter of weeks. My mother, who appeared genuinely sorry, suspected it was due to some intrinsic Protestant weakness. Within a few months, she began to suggest that Moira had a Godgiven second chance in which she could, this time, do things properly.

Moira took it badly. Her sorrow over Franz's death compounded her indignation over mother's suggestions. I doubt that the denouement, which was approaching with the speed of Moira's Mini-

Morris that Sunday morning, was inspired solely by spite but you never know the germ of developments.

Moira's phone call may only have been a plea for moral support. Later she told me "I wanted you there so Mum wouldn't think she'd imagined it all next day." But there may also have been an unconfessed worry about the news' effect.

Which brings us to the big scene played in undertones. Brendan Mangin had remained close to Moira and Franz after giving him instructions. Mangin's sympathy had consoled Moira on Franz's death. She, in turn, had been understanding with Mangin when he left the priesthood. A blind man could have seen the likely development of that relationship but I rarely met Moira and my mother could not have conceived the possibility.

For my mother, priesthood was impressed as an indelible character on the soul. Once a priest always a priest. If you were a priest, the only alternative was to spoil. You could not return to a pre-priestly state. "Butter, when it goes bad, doesn't turn back to milk," one of our parish priests used to say, "it just gets more and more rancid."

In fact, my mother was so innocent about the possibilities of the relationship that Mangin, who arrived with Moira that Sunday, could not find an opening for his announcement. Mangin is a hefty fellow with strong features: generous mouth, towering forehead and I wish I had the gold dust it would take to fill his beaky nose. Franz had been built like a wardrobe: Moira liked big men, perhaps because she found they are easy to manage. Mangin, for all his powerful build, was a nervous as a kitten, poor fellow, possibly because his mother had threatened that his leaving the priesthood would cause her a stoke. She was still hale but he had aged fifteen years in the three since he had taken that decision and his blithe spirit had drooped.

"I suppose you'll wonder why I've come here Mrs Twomey," he said after the preliminaries, a piece of mother's chocolate sponge sagging from his fingers.

"Always glad to see you Father." Every now and again, my mother disconcerted him by dropping into the familiar form of address.

"Thank you — but I meant you'd wonder why I'd come here with Moira."

He perched on the edge of the lounge chair as if scalded.

My mother had no patience with beating about the bush. "Moira can always do with some sound advice," she said, "and she's deaf to me."

"Mum, for goodness sake listen to what Brendan is trying to tell you." Moira was exasperated but amused. She was always called the spitting image of mother. Despite mother's threee score and ten years, they were only odd white stands in her black hair. She and Moira shared an almost masculine proudness in their bony faces. But I noticed a new quality about Moira: her lipstick was too bright; in contrast, her cheeks were too pallid; and her nails, lacquered in a garish red, were longer than I had ever seen them. I was reminded of what I had read abut German naval officers before the first world war. They refrained from cutting the nail of the left-hand little finger until the day when the British Navy would be defeated. That was to be The Day,

Der Tag. They had missed out but, it occurred to me, this was Der Tag for Moira.

"Take your hand away from your face Moira, you'll ruin it. Of course I can hear what he's saying — I'm not doddering, whatever my children think. As long as we get to the point."

In my mind, a camera clicked at that moment before mother got to the point, before her vulnerability became evident. The tableau consisted of Mangin, beady with perspiration although it was a mild if sunny morning, frightened of the effect he had on females, mistakingly trusting words to help him; my mother confident that the battles she had fought were all part of the good fight, her love expressed mainly as an impatience with Moira; and, most ambiguous of all in that group bathed by champagne sunlight, if we can exclude the cameraman, Moira, about to play her ace but, perhaps, concerned at the possible effects of her victory.

"Mrs Twomey," Mangin began hesitantly, "what would you say if Moira were to marry again?"

Mother must have cottoned on then. Although she had been looking at Mangin, now she refocused.

"If she found the right man," said my mother, implying it was unlikely, "I'd be happy."

I felt like kicking the tripod aside, whisking away the black cloth and telling Mangin to start again.

"What would you say if I said . . ." Both women should have sundered him for ineptness. Mangin had been a happy-go-lucky priest. If there were no more penitents at his confessional, he was capable of sticking his head out like a jack-in-the-box and calling to those waiting for the other priest "Any takers?" Some of his sermons were worth hearing because he linked the Gospel with current affairs but now his tongue seemed addicted to hypothetical clauses.

Moira was watching mother, not Mangin. And mother, instead of launching one of her broadsides, was mute. Invited to speak, she said nothing, an utter rout. Always pallid, she blanched. Her lips thinned. Had she suffered the stroke Mrs Mangin had threatened?

I realized I should divert attention. I had seen what was in the offing but nevertheless was flummoxed. I would like to have asked questions but instead offered to get beer from the fridge for a celebratory drink.

It gave me a respite. God, I thought, as I extracted those frosted beer cans, what a comeuppance. Godgiven chance for a proper marriage with a Catholic . . . and she comes up with Mangin. What could be more Catholic than an ex-priest?

The conversation was stilted. The whine of an electric mower reached us from a nearby garden. We were all anxious to avoid anything which would further upset mother who sat as if surviving in another sphere. And, despite myself, I found the conversational terrain with an ex-priest who is to become your brother-in-law is mined.

Moira was chattering about Gretel finding a black cocker pup near the house of the friends with whom she was staying when in walked Frank like a zombie, presumably back from Mass. He listlessly greeted his mother, reluctantly acknowledged Mangin's presence, then slumped beside me as if he had been walking for miles.

166

Mangin enquired about Frank's studies. Automatically he had disqualified himself: Frank not only loathed being introduced to adults, he hated all conventional queries after health, school or likely future occupation. Whichever way you approached him, you ran into a roadblock.

"Frank, my boy." It was a surprise to hear my mother, as if we had assumed that she had lost the power of speech. Indeed all of a sudden she had the slow enunciation, the spent eye of a ninety-year-old "Do you know your mother intends to marry Father Mangin?"

A broadside when it was presumed the galleon was abandoned and adrift. A desperate last throw for the younger generation.

Frank gave a basilisk stare at Mangin but most adults in those days were subject to his death-ray looks. Apparently mother had calculated aright that it was news to Frank, and unwelcome. But she was mistaken to think he would be upset that his mother was marrying Mangin after he had left the priesthood. No, it was just that Frank distrusted all priests, even those that were not spoiled.

"You're not a priest anymore, are you?" asked Frank from deep within his defence perimeter.

"No, I'm in insurance these days."

"That's not much of a change," said Frank with a rare flash of humour which Mangin did not appreciate.

"What do you have to get married for?" Frank asked his mother coldly.

"I'll talk to you about that later," said Moira, discomfited for once.

Frank gave the impression that the matter, while

distasteful, concerned him only marginally. He was already launched on the trajectory which was to take him through university on scholarships.

The news concerned Gretel, however, who suffers the strains and stresses of Mangin adjusting to Moira and this-life insurance problems.

Mangin has never recovered the patina he had as a progressive priest. His opinions seem unexceptional now that he is no longer a maverick. These days he recaptures his buoyancy only shen tanked. He has begun to switch jobs with frequency. Although Mangin's friends cannot stand her, Moira, always competent, keeps that ship afloat.

Anyway, they may still be young enough to make their accommodations. My sympathies were, ultimately, with my mother for it was too late for her to do other than suffer the irony of Moira marrying Mangin.

She did not remain stricken in her chair after Frank withdrew that morning to return to his Marxist masters. Realizing her last salvo had fallen astray, she still had the grace to murmur she had things to give Moira for the wedding.

Mother made an effort to treat Mangin well, probably regretting that she had not been kinder to Franz and fearing that Mangin might, likewise, vanish from one moment to the next. But, in fact, it was mother who slipped away last year, having been subdued and distant ever since the morning of Der Tag. I'm sure that, for all her efforts to think otherwise, until her dying day Mangin remained for her a priest living in unspeakable concubinage. That he remained a practising Catholic cut no ice with her. She had been cast in a mould before the Council and to break the mould was to break her.

She schooled herself to call him Brendan but, as she became more distracted towards the end, she began calling him Father Brendan, nonplussing both him and Moira to a degree which would have delighted her when she was more combative. On her death bed, a new priest came from the parish church to give extreme unction. Moira sent him away when she found his name was Brendan, for fear of possible confusion. The parish priest arrived just in time.

And her son, whose hand on the imaginary camera had trembled as Moira's future husband put his case? He was seeing the scene through his mother's as yet uncomprehending eyes but wondering desperately if it were possible to amend it. A negative film would have been the best solution with Moira as black as a Hottentot and, of course, her mother the same colour. But Brendan, even if as black as sin, would remain an ex-priest, there was no getting away from that. For my mother the shot could not be juggled into acceptable form and I still see the scene through her eyes as well as mine.

But you were asking after the cameraman. He continues to live in his mother's house rather than accept an invitation to join Moira and Brendan. Take Frank's place, don't you know. Kind of them to make the offer. It's a toss-sup whether the Twomeys are tightknit or just tight. Of course, joining Moira and Brendan would allow immediate sale of mother's house with half the proceeds going to big sis. But didn't I earn the right to go on living here while nursing mother: you could say there was almost a reveral of roles between Moira and myself. And mother could still be enjoying her home herself if it hadn't been for Der Tag.

They expect me to pay them rent. But how can you pay rent if you're not earning regularly — something every now and again in the film business but God knows it's chancy; you have to make the right friends. I'd certainly surprise them if I found a girl, Catholic or not, who set up house here: Der Tag in reverse, almost a posthumous evening of scores for mother. Meet and just, but I'm taking my time about it. I know enough about false starts.

The Importance of Being Henry

"I MET A BLOODY fantastic character last night in the Marble bar."

Clyde Burton propped himself on his elbow, looking down on Melinda who he had been caressing while recouping his forces.

"Bewdy. Straight out of Lawson — the hat, the cavalry twill trousers, the far-away eyes. Must find the descripton of him."

He rummaged in the bookcase beneath a long window. Outside, the blue of Sirius Cove heightened that of the garden's hydrangea heads. Clyde's pubic hair gleamed red in the sunlight lapping his slack stomach.

The one sheet on the bed was as rucked as the harbour. Melinda punched her pillow into shape and rolled on her side away from Clyde. He was often irritatingly randy of a morning. But Sundays were worst of all as neither had to go to university where Clyde lectured on literature and Melinda was completing her arts degree.

She suspected his Sunday morning performances were dictated only by a desire to prove a point. His breaking away to seek Lawson when the surf of her feeling was rising rankled. She wanted to dump him, splinter his surfboard. She guessed he had an opportunity to do something he preferred: dazzle her with his pedantry.

"Here it is," exulted Clyde, falling on the bed with the thick Lawson volume, "this is him — listen: tall and straight yet — rather straighter than he had been — dressed in a comfortable, serviceable sac suit of 'saddle-tweed', and wearing a new sugar-loaf, cabbage-tree hat, he looked over the hurrying street people calmly as though they were sheep of which he was not in charge, and which were not likely to get 'boxed with his. Not the worst way in which to regard the world."

"There's no mention of cavalry twill pants," objected Melinda, unwilling to play along with Clyde. "You must have been duped by the Marble bar decor — or had a vision when you tottered past the Lawson bookshop there."

"You're awake early this morning Fatso — even if it sounds you slept badly." Fatso, Clyde's surrogate for an endearment, underlined her slimnesss. "It's him to a T — uncanny. You'll have to believe it."

"Who the hell is he?"

"Lawson calls him Joe Wilson."

"Didn't you ask him his name?"

"You wouldn't expect it to be Joe Wilson would you? I've taught you the XYZ but I see we'll have to go back to the ABC. Writers pinch characteristics not names — if it's the same name, it must be another person, if you savvy. He gave me his card. Got it somewhere — I wasn't tanked enough to lose that."

He fumbled among his clothes draped over a bedside chair, stirring an earth-acidy smell, his.

"Joseph Burgess," he read from the card, "halfway there — if you pull that cracker, Wilson could well topple out. You'll see for yourself Mel," he promised, "at the farewell party."

"You going somewhere?" Melinda asked dryly.

"*He's* sailing for England — I might have missed him altogether."

That afternoon Melinda, who had not touched Lawson since secondary school, read the Joe Wilson stories for the first time. She realized then that they had been completed in 1901.

"Are you having me on?" she challenged Clyde as she dressed for the farewell party, "Lawson's Joe Wilson already had grey hairs."

"He's got a whole head of them now," Clyde replied as if it proved his point. As his student, and when she had first moved in with him, she had accepted such statements as appropriate for a genius.

Melinda confessed she liked the way Lawson talked about Joe's relations with his wife Mary. It was the sort of thing she would like to experience and write herself whereas the models Clyde admired had always seemed unattainable. She read a passage: "Then we sat, side by side, on the edge of the verandah, and talked more than we'd done for years — and there was a good deal of 'Do you remember'in it — and I think we got to understand each other better that night. "And at last Mary said, 'Do you know, Joe, why, I feel tonight just — just like I did the day we were married!' And somehow I had that strange, shy sort of feeling too."

"Now you're having *me* on," Clyde protested. "Didn't know you went for sentimental ratshit."

"It's sweet," said Melinda and he could not tell whether she was serious, "like this other ending:

'You've got the scar on the bridge of your nose still' said Mary, kissing it, 'and' — as if she'd just noticed it for the first time — 'why! you hair is greyer than ever', and she pulled down my head, and her fingers began to go through my hair as in the days of old. And when we got to the hotel in Cudgegong, she made me have a bath and lie down on the bed and go to sleep. And when I awoke, late in the afternoon, she was sitting by my side, smoothing my hair."

"The sickest thing about Henry," said Clyde as if dictating a definitive statement, "is his fear of women — most of his characters have been done down by women. You've got those tough bushmen huddled around campfires congratulating each other on escaping from womanly wiles. Pussy fear stalks the bush."

"I don't know," Melinda responded lightly," Joe Wilson always regrets he didn't treat Mary better."

"That's the other side of the medal-castrating guilt complex. Should've known *you'd* like it. A born castrator."

Melinda asked why, if Clyde destested Lawson, he was so excited by the previous night's meeting.

"The point about a minor writer like Lawson," Clyde answered, "is that we know more about his characters than he does. We can see Lawson's characters are alienated but he can't. Burgess proves what I always suspected about Joe Wilson."

Melinda knew Clyde saw through everyone, regularly. Laser eyes. Right through and out the other side with never a pause. His pub discovery, she guessed, would be a source of anecdotes, briefly holding boredom at bay. But it had stirred her imagination, even if she was wary of letting Clyde know.

"Did you ask his wife's name?"

"Didn't get a chance. That'll be a test though, won't it?"

They both had it in mind when they arrived, in the most conventional clothes they could muster, at the farewell party. But Burgess's wife was Anna, a Singapore Chinese. On meeting her, Clyde gave Melinda a so-much-for-my-theory look. For Melinda, Burgess was almost as big a surprise as Anna. His manner was so English, he was a straightbacked, Alec Guiness-type who would keep up a brave front even while silently crumbling. Melinda guessed hardening of the arteries caused the beyond-the-sheep look of his celluloid-blue eyes.

The venerable, well-heeled guests seemed impervious to the broken mirror sky, the well of harbour directly below the cliff-like apartment building. It reminded Clyde of Venice where baskets were lowered from apartments directly to boats to be filled with fish.

"Why didn't you tell me he comes on like a Pom?" Melinda challenged Clyde as they helped themselves to the buffet.

"Wanted to ignore contrary evidence," admitted Clyde, tired now of his short flight of imagination, bored by the company of old fogeys.

"Complicating, not contrary," corrected Melinda, "Joe Wilson shifted to London and admired the Poms. I can just see him blending with the background."

"That's fancy not imagination — don't let it

seduce you," advised Clyde as he drifted back to the group around Burgess.

Melinda attached herself to Anna who, excluded from the men's conversation, showed her the rest of the apartment.

Clyde, for a last scruple, wanted to pose Burgess the question he had not asked in the Marble bar: "Did you know a writerman named Lawson?"

But it was difficult to corner Burgess. From his conversation, Clyde understood that Burgess had returned to his native land to inspect country property but was happy to be sailing from brassy Sydney. When Clyde finally posed his question, Burgess was drunk on gin and tonic. His chalk white cheeks were flushed and he was fighting a stiff-upper-lipped battle for control of his speech.

"Lawson? Of course." His gaze shifted from the far horizon only he discerned to Clyde who could have been one of the sheep with whom he preferred not to be boxed. "Was at his funeral — never seen anything like it, not a dry eye in Sydney."

Again he looked beyond Clyde who suspected Burgess was a compulsive liar whose fixed stare was calculated to discountance facts.

Clyde's voice became querelous: "But did you know him, earlier, in the outback?"

"Small selector wasn't he?" said Burgess loftily, "can't remember he was ever on my property — but you never know."

He resumed reminiscing about Slim, a bosom mate of his Burma days, and the necessity of constant quinine supplies.

Should have his pith helmet on out here in the colonies, thought Clyde as he sought Melinda. He calculated they could still make it to a writers' rort in Balmain. Together, they farewelled Burgess.

"Young man, I'd like to present you with this," said Burgess, tipsily, offering Clyde his plate on which a monogram was visible beneath lobster shell and mayonnaise debris.

Clyde, embarrassed, said he would not know what to do with it.

"Nor do I," responded Burgess who seemed to discover then the plate between his hands. "You could inscribe on it, young lady," he added with an effort , "'ware of the demon drink."

"Total loss," was Clyde's comment as they descended from the top floor apartment. Melinda stroked the night air as they walked the harbourfront towards Clyde's car. She looked over her shoulder, then pulled Clyde around just in time to see Burgess, from his apartment window, pensively cast a plate into the dark. It arched fulsomely before slicing the moon-slimed water.

Melinda moaned.

"During the Renaissance, a Roman family used to do that with gold plates," Clyde lectured. "Throw them into the Tiber — they had nets underwater to catch them. Designed to impress the guests. You impressed?"

"Must be the last plate of the set he used with Mary," Melinda drawled.

"Come off it, Fatso. The name's Burgess not Borges."

"No, it *could* be, Clyde." A little girl being wilful.

"Ho-hum. Wishing won't make it so. 'O'Grady

says' must be your favourite game — you work by opposites."

He backed the car, wondering why she persisted. She noticed how his powerful shoulders were hunched as if he wore a thich sweater although he had only a light jacket. His body was thickening fast just as his attitudes were jelling hard.

"So Joe Wilson became a Pom."

"He even liked the climate," she insisted, "stood up for the English — there's that line in 'Joe Wilson in England': 'The only solid help I ever got was from an Englishman'. Can't you see Joe'd fit in? Distinguished: they couldn't label him as a rough Aussie. He's acquired the real English touch: he looks through you without seeing you."

Clyde was surprised by Melinda but seemed prepared to humour her.

"How did Joe Wilson get to Burma though? I should have asked him if he'd run into Eric Blair. Or how it was by the old Moulmein pagoda? That's more his period."

"That's easy — once you make the transfer to England, one colony resembles another. All good masculine company."

Suddenly Clyde was irritated by Melinda's febrile talk. He teased her for her freeflow fancy at his friend's in Balmain but she did not rise to the bait. For the first time she felt immune to his sallies.

The following day Clyde exhumed a wide-ranging essay which he believed would, if ever completed, unlock Patrick White. And wrote. But feared at times that he was lost in a desert without contact with either the living or the dead.

As he presumed Lawson had been left behind, he

was testy when the subject surfaced again on Tuesday morning. His nerves were frayed by the scorching nor'westerly.

"Jesus!" Clyde had exploded, exasperated by Melinda's recalcitrance in a discussion about Aborigines, "with the best will in the world, it still seems to me women keep their brains between their legs."

Melinda was accustomed to such pleasantries but this time leapt on it as an updated version of Joe Wilsons's "I often think it's a great pity that women haven't brains."

"Next you'll prove I'm Joe Wilson."

"Never. Joe Burgess is enough."

"Or too much. You're not going to keep that up, are you?"

"I'm going to write a story about it."

Clyde swung his legs off the bed and sat, sensing he had to stop Melinda before she went further. It was getting beyond a joke.

"And have him livng in the outback with his Chink wife — that's how the Bully got its pink page, I bet: saw red."

"But she came after Mary, of course: Mary couldn't get used to England or the English. Didn't you even take that trick?"

Clyde looked narrow-eyed at Melinda. He suspected she was becoming a Burgess-like liar and it made him insecure.

"Cool it Mel" was his advice, "I was excited about him as a talking point — not to be taken seriously."

"She *told* me, Clyde," Melinda insisted, "Burgess's first wife was Mary."

"It's a fine old name," Clyde responded although

he was shaken, "Joe Wilson's wife didn't patent it."

"And whatsmore," she sat and he felt her breasts were bald heads about to butt him, " she showed me things he's kept from that first marriage."

"A doubly buggy in the bedroom?"

"No," she said more calmly, like a marksman with his victim's low forehead in his sights, "but a little Wilcox and Gibbs sewing machine."

Clyde was at a loss.

"You don't even remember the stories — what he gave her as a wedding present in 'Water Them Geraniums'."

"How do you know it was the same model?" He knew he was dead but would not lie down. "And you want to begin your brilliant career writing that story? A cock and bull," he said and then repeated it to himself as if listening for a faint coda, "a cock and bull . . ." He rose and returned the Lawson volume to the bookcase. He would take a close look at it as soon as Melinda left for the university.

"Sure," said Melinda, "why not? I can start, can't I?" And knew, at last, that she could. The story was shaping itself swiftly now, it had enough kick to reassure her it was alive.

"No one's stopping you Fatso, but you'll go bung. You need not only female fancy but a plausible story — oh yes, oh dear yes, you must tell a story. You'll have to believe me."

The only time he's used "dear" with me, Melinda realized and recognized it was an echo. Nevertheless, she sprang bouyantly from the bed. Before leaving for university she would water the blue hydrangeas by the front gate. Otherwise, in the searing wind, the delicate plants would wilt.

Circe in Capri

AS SHE SAT awaiting her coffee in Capri's main
piazza, Sandy rehearsed Derek's phone call which
had woken her at dawn. Desperate for his earplugs.
She could imagine the fine leather of Derek's face
sagging under his sincere eyes if he had not been
able to sleep. Make him look ten years older,
suitable for distinguished *roué* roles.

She had asked him if the premiere of Marta's film
was a success. Sandy's position as Derek's secretary
depended on a revival of Marta's fortunes. "A
knock-out": the ebb and flow in the line washed
any enthusiasm from his voice but it had
strengthened as he asked "How's the magnum O.
going, baby?"

To hear that first thing was enough to foul her
day, thought Sandy as she sipped her coffee after
having despatched the earplugs. Straw-hatted
tourists and preening cats were the only life in the
piazza. Sandy, still jarred by the phone call, did not
feel up to transcribing more of Derek's tapes. In
them he talked tirelessly about his country-town
boyhood, his precocious Sydney amatory ex-
periences, his radio success, the stir when he took to
kissing women who interviewed him, the swathe he
cut in London, his first adventure films, his first
three wives, every narcissistic detail, in fact, until he

had met Marta. The gently whirring tape caught it all and Derek would tell Sandy to throw in the commas and full stops as she typed.

An account of Derek's amatory adventures could interest his dwindling female fans. But instead of simply telling the story of a wild colonial boy, he wanted to be taken seriously by critics. Instead of relying on accounts of laying Hollywood lovelies, he introduced shopworn sociology and modish anguish.

Something other than the irregular salary must have kept Sandy at the boring task of transcribing these meanderings, either Derek or Capri's spell. She had sought the island as a refuge a week after disembarking in Naples. A law student had first identified Capri for her when he pointed to a hovercraft arrowing towards the island. 'We're like that ship," he said, "in the air — floating. A mirage. Naples looks solid to you but we feel the shiver always. It's old Vesuvio."

She had not know what he meant: she could not linger long enough in the tight-knit streets where all life seemed to sizzle like the food in open-air frying pans. Everything was mixed with everything else; people made a perpetual feast of their poverty. Sandy felt she had discovered how life must have been before it was sorted into neat, stagnant compartments. In the previous ports of call from Sydney, she had been a curious tourist but here she was looking for something of her own. It was the sudden expansion of perspectives, the earnest of an alternative which exhilarated her.

But her travelling companion Margot fell ill and, putty-faced, uttering dire warnings about the local food, flew to London. Next, after selecting a pair of new shoes, Sandy found her purse had been lifted and she suspected the law student who had attached himself to her, practising his rudimentary English. Maybe that was what he had meant with his talk of mirages: all Italians were actors, she reminded herself, people who play with the emotions. She had taken a ferry to Capri which she felt must have been set offshore for those who otherwise would be submerged by Neapolitan life's lava flow and, in a bar off the main piazza, had met Derek. He managed the boyish smile which had disarmed tougher damsels than Sandy.

"Sometimes he seems lost despite all his put-on," Sandy write to her mother when she had settled at the villa as Derek's secretary. Occasionally she wanted to ruffle his unruly hair. The closest they came to intimacy, however, was when they spoke about their Sydney childhoods: they could have been two boys swapping memories of climbing cliff faces, swimming off the rocks, exploring Taronga Park zoo. Derek would call her "Dig"; at other times, that mellifluous voice with the neutral, international accent took a distant tone. The abrupt shifts between indifference and friendliness were like the treatment used to induce breakdown among concentration camp prisoners.

Yet sometimes, as now lingering over her coffee, Sandy imagined herself as Derek's fifth wife. Of course they would no longer enjoy Marta's villa, but they could return to Sydney. Derek confessed that he made only brief visits home because "they're so swift to sweep you under the carpet". But Sandy saw that, as people would soon be walking on Derek wherever he was, it would be better for him to be a returned celebrity in Sydney, perhaps champion of an Australian film industry.

The premiere of Marta's film was such a success that her slide to oblivion ceased. Weeklies carried filmshots of her emerging from the waves, gripping handrails which descend the rocks at Positano: pearls of water glistening on her shoulders, the waves' swell less oceanic than that of her breasts manfully upthrust by a canny bikini. Some shots showed her neck arched powerfully, in others she smiled upwards, strong teeth dazzling, incipient double-chin taut.

Her fortune had always come from the sea even though she could barely swim a stroke. When she had first arrived in Italy from Sweden she had invariably been photographed at swimming pools. Such a variety of entrancing bathing caps which never got wet. Or bikinis which could not have been pared finer. Now she was re-emerging as a goddess from the sea.

Once again Marta believed that, if she left the villa, photographers might snap her. It may have been this which made her irritable with Riccardo. Magazines used to refer to him as Marta's body-guard. Then she had managed to find him a small film role, her cleverest seduction, and he became known as her actor-friend. For a long time no one had been interested enough to uncover that she had picked up a Capri fisherman as her *cicisbeo*. But it was better to keep it hidden now that her reputation as a sex goddess might revive. After all, she and Derek were supposed to represent an amalgam of red-hot passion and, although Derek was fading fast from the scene, any boyfriend would have to be glossy if she wanted to avoid being lynched by the movie magazines.

This could have been the reason she was bitchier than ever after the premiere. She became more domineering because of the renewed attention, but fretful for fear it might be short-lived. In fact, it faded as the box-office returns did not confirm the hopes raised by the premiere.

The servants suffered most. The aged couple who tended the house had a holy terror of Signora Marta. If she identified errors in the bills they presented, she presumed they were intentional, but she doled out money for running expenses in such minute quantities that they must have found a way of multipying it. After the premier she increased her vigilance as if anticipating domestic sabotage. The servants looked with concern at Marta's gun hanging against the dining-room wall as if she might turn it on them as she did against anyone who wandered on her property's seafront.

Marta treated Derek's big-boned secretary Sandy as a higher-grade servant. She ignored her as far as possible but now ordered her to buy sheaves of papers and magazines daily: Marta had rediscovered her interest in every crumb of film-world gossip. She was kind only to animals. There were birds, rabbits, tortoises and, above all, cats. Her prodigality with them was one of the few things which could upset Derek's Olympian calm.

"Oh, dice it Marta," he would complain as if her

demonstrativeness was to spite him, "I'll give you a swan if you have to have it." Only the taut lines around his mouth, like those of a sheriff looking down the outlaw's gunbarrel, betrayed the strain.

"A swan would be nice, Derek, but where would I put it? " Marta would reply, sprawled on the couch under her luxuriant, favourite Siamese cat Sirikit.

One morning Derek added a threat: "People can catch asthma from cats."

Always something of a health crank, Derek's recent cultural escalation had made him an expert on psychosomatic ailments. He stopped playing draughts with Riccardo long enough to fix a precocious Martini and stand over Marta explaining why cats could induce asthma.

She closed her eyes, continuing to fondle the cat, until Derek returned to the draught board; then she flung off a startled Sirikit, screaming "You want to spoil this too."

Marta had half-blamed Derek for the decline of her career, just as originally she had associated him with its success. Partly because she had further to fall, she had suffered more than Derek from the downturn. She had reacted with bursts of desperate energy during which she dieted, made sallies to Rome, sought contacts and publicity. But mainly it had been a slow slide to apathy before the opportunity offered by the latest film.

On Marta, the toll of neglect had been more evident than with Derek. Plumpness hid the cheekbones which had been shapely as staves, her blonde hair was not only dyed but dead, and Derek had always found her skin too white: as he said, more turnip than Swede. Even her purple eyes had faded, eyes that had once convinced a producer to abandon black-and-white for technicolour. They had made Derek catch his breath when he first met Marta. Now they merely daunted him because they promised something Marta never delivered. When lived with, their dry-ice quality proved merely self-centred.

No noise was permitted before the appearance of Marta about eleven each morning. Creams smothered her face, a cap held her once golden hair as she ate her way through slice after slice of rye bread with honey, prosperous grapefruits, and cartons of yoghurt, all dietary items but in outrageous quantities.

Afternoons and nights were for Riccardo. Some afternoons they would retire to the roof terrace, sun-drenched and strewn with rubber mattresses. Capri gossip had it that Marta took the sun nude; what Riccardo did was a subject for lewd speculation. There was a tacit invitation for Derek to join them but he dictated for Sandy. Other afternoons the rite changed. Riccardo would take Marta out in his boat, lazing around the island or exploring the gulf. Often they returned only after dusk and ate on the patio by candlelight. Derek would probably be out, drinking himself silly, while Marta would be grateful to Riccardo and generous with the beseeching cats. But she clashed with Riccardo when, after almost abandoning hope of a premiere follow-up, she received an offer from Hollywood, where she had been noticed rising from the waves.

Perhaps Riccardo wanted her to take him along and she knew that was to be avoided at all costs. Or perhaps, as happened every so often, she just had to fulminate Riccardo whom Derek called "the lightning conductor".

As Derek saw the scene, it was one of Marta's best. He had returned early from a bar-crawl with his stomach emitting signals which, because of his recent medical reading, he interpreted ominously. He reclined on a cane lounge at the far end of the patio, drowning himself in Dvorak's "From the New World" symphony. As usual he wore dark glasses although he had to protect his soulful eyes only from the new moon.

He saw Marta wildly gesticulate, but imagined she was recounting a story. However when she crashed a wine bottle on the Vietri tiles, scattering her court of cats, Derek discreetly lowered his record-player's volume. Effective sotto-voce, Riccardo was no match for Marta in a shouting match. Marta was shouting *"gigolo schifoso"* and he responded angrily. Any answer, Derek knew, was a mistake although silence also would enrage Marta. She would seize the reply, twist its meaning, link it with imagined past offences and present it whole as evidence of a long-nutured hate.

She had gathered a few of the cowering cats and was accusing Riccardo, who held his nut-like head between his hands, of exasperating her to the point where she had frightened them. If only she captured this dramatic sense in front of the movie camera, where she was usually as bare and wooden as a coathanger, thought Derek, she would not need to fear her fate. She entered the lounge to examine some supposed cut to Sirikit from flying glass, berating Riccardo for not loving animals. "Marta,

Marta, you don't let me say a word," was his losing answer, overwhelmed by her ringing *"ignorante maleducato!"*

When she denounced Italians as vermin unaccountably blessed with a paradisal country, Derek knew they had reached the last act. Marta's contempt, as always, stirred Riccardo's patriotic bile. Derek considered Riccardo reacted more strongly to such comments than to Marta's personal abuse because he had an accurate opinion of his own worth. Usually a blazing beauty in attack, at Riccardo's response Marta's face contorted. She seized the nearest object, a heavy transistor radio, which she raised high before smashing it to the floor. B.B.C. wiped out, thought Derek resignedly. She advanced on Riccardo, screaming. If she doesn't want to take her buck to Hollywood, that's up to her, but I'm damned if I'm going to resume my role in our oversexed duo, Derek told himself, hiding behind Dvorak and his dark glasses. He looked forward to returning to Hollywood in his own right if only he could do the trick with magnum O.

Women friends came to console Riccardo's wife, Maddalena, but she did not feel the need. She had bought a television and, after her daylong sewing, would watch it until the close of transmission. The visitors' comments sometimes spoiled her favourite programs.

It was a pleasant way of awaiting Riccardo's return. He had already returned twice and she knew he must come again. Even though he treated her badly and swore he was no longer her husband, Maddalena was serene. In the eyes of the law he was always her husband and, through the parish priest, she was trying to convince the authorities to deny Marta entry into Italy. But reliance on the law was not the source of her serenity. Rather she trusted Riccardo whom she continued to describe as a fine youngster although he, like her, was pushing forty. "As good as gold," she claimed, "it's only because that woman has cast a spell on him." She was as indifferent as a nun to the blandishments of the postman Tiberio whose concern when it rained was never for his bare head but for his letters.

Although Maddalena believed that the spell would eventually be broken, she was surprised, on return from market, to find Riccardo on their bed the day after his clash with Marta. To Maddalena he looked defenceless, exhausted like an overgrown boy about to wake from an evil spell. She sliced purple eggplants and began to prepare his lunch but it was sunset before he awoke.

He was gruff, on the defensive and ate the elaborate dinner as if he were doing her a favour. The television program saved them from having to confront one another and, as it terminated, Riccardo yawned cavernously. Maddalena understood that he needed to sleep immediately.

The next day was easier. Riccardo was less tense, as if he were no longer playing an exacting role. He was accepted by the neighbours who, whatever their private comments, told Maddalena he was merely one of the victims of the rich who invaded Capri. The feast day of the Madonna of the Fishermen followed. In the evening, Riccardo and Maddalena joined the procession as if they had been together since the priest who led it married them. It concluded at the end of the quay under a sinuous, blue-bulbed M which stood for Madonna but for Riccardo could have meant also Marta or Maddalena and possibly both. Afterwards, with other couples, they watched the festive lights, red, yellow and green, stretch swaying on the slick sea and a dazzling, deafening fireworks display. Maddalena felt they had never been separated.

The next afternoon, her child of hope died. As they sat talking after lunch, Riccardo mentioned that with a little ready cash he could exchange his fishing boat for a much better one. With the greater returns from the fishing boat, he argued, she would no longer have to work during the summer for Neapolitans in an Anacapri villa. But she knew it was merely the savings from that work he was after. He was sorry to ask so soon after his return, but otherwise the bargain would be snapped-up . . .

"Don't go on and on," said Maddalena, moving to the drawer where she kept her pay-to-bearer bank passbook, heavy-legged but unable to resist.

"I can't stand that martyred look: go and live with stupid Tiberio if you have to."

She put the passbook in his hand, saying he could go.

"That's all you think of me!" Riccardo might have learnt his reponses on the set of one of Marta's films.

"Let her treat you like her pigs." There were

rumours that Marta had pigs in the lower part of her property. Maddalena had her back against a wall as sallow as her face.

Riccardo, congested with willed anger, slammed his chair against the table but stuffed the passbook in his hip pocket. "Spite's all you've got. God knows, I've tried to make a go of it but you want to drown me — you won't see me again."

Of course she saw him again. Most afternoons when she crossed the piazza to take the funicular home he was lounging on the belvedere with his no-good friends: Carmelo who had run off with a German strip-teaser and returned briefly each summer while his wife displayed herself on the Italian circuit; Andrea who found it hard to get work as a waiter after being imprisoned for peddling drugs; Adriano who had had a heavy summer with a middle-aged American tourist and had made the mistake of following her to the States.

Tourists who passed were sharply assessed by all except Riccardo who seemed melancholy, distract-ed — which, for Maddalena, was further proof that he was not corrupt. He avoided her eye.

Maddalena knew that the stranger would disappear just as suddenly as she had come. Even now she was away from the island and perhaps would never return.

Later Derek thought of it as Black Friday but always added a mental footnote: dark precedes the dawn. He had received an irritating letter from his literary agent who claimed there was no market for what he had seen of the autobiography. He advised

Derek to cut the crap and get Marta on the scene as early as possible. Derek had intended to finish the saga of self before his last pyrrhic victory but unless he included Marta, apparently, there was little hope of regaining freedom from her.

Derek had been pacing the lounge room re-reading the typescript aloud and watching over his dark glasses for reactions from Sandy, coiled in a cane chair, when Marta arrived. There must have been some hitch in Hollywood for her reappearance was premature but Derek's sixth sense warned him not to inquire. Sensing that he would have to tag along with Marta for longer than he had hoped, he improvised a present for her recent unremarked birthday: a record of Leonard Bernstein conducting Prokofiev's fifth symphony which Derek had bought for himself but did not enjoy.

The last thing Marta wanted to be reminded of was her age, Prokofiev was hardly her line of country, and she guessed that the present was, in any case, phoney. But all the same it broke her up. While Derek fixed her drinks, she launched into a rambling "I said, he said" account of her trip. To her surprise, Sandy saw two old pros discussing their trade. Derek did not even see the funny side of it when Marta said she had stalked out once it became clear that they wanted her to play not the sex goddess but, and she twisted her mouth on the unwelcome word, "her mother".

Marta's self-assurance gave way to a rare defence-lessness, perhaps because of fatigue, and Derek seemed to unfold. Sandy found an excuse to leave them alone for she felt an intruder. "They'll become maudlin before long," she predicted, keeping at bay the suspicion that once they had been mutually responsive.

The next day it would have been hard to tell that Marta had ever been away: when, with face besmeared, she descended late in the morning, she had again acquired her carapace of self-sufficiency and Derek, unflurried, retreated to his own territory. Marta made a fuss of Sirikit, who had pined away during her absence, before she dressed to go out in a blue shantung trouser suit revealing a figure which the kindliest gossip writer could only describe as prosperous.

She had not returned by lunchtime. Sandy and Derek had reached the Sicilian oranges and olives salad when Marta entered with Riccardo.

It was a replay: Riccardo unshaven, slightly abashed, hands trembling as if he were a sacrificial victim, or it might have been in anticipation of pleasure. Marta, ready to amuse herself with her catch, was impervious to the strained atmosphere.

Sandy checked that the gun was still against the wall but Marta could not have been more the huntress if she had taken it with her. Sandy's imagination stopped short when she tried to see Marta prising Riccardo from his fellow loungers who clung together as tightly as coral polyps. But she speculated that they might be like the peasants who waited around village squares for landowners to select them as labourers. And Marta, Sandy decided while trying to impale a black olive, would have been as assured as any contractor. It nauseated Sandy for the servants had told her of Maddalena's devotion to Riccardo.

After lunch, dominated by Marta's chatter which

was as full of bright, disparate objects as a magpie's nest, she retired to the roof terrace with Riccardo. Derek listened morosely to some blues, pouring glasses of straight whisky which he drank slowly but without pause. His only gesture towards Sandy was to hold up the bottle every so often as an invitation. Terrified, she nursed her tot.

To her relief, after emptying the whisky bottle, he told Sandy he would take a nap and advised her to do likewise. They found each other again towards six. Derek had slept off the effect of the whisky and, although helping himself to a carafe of red wine while trying to organize races between the tortoises, he seemed serene. As they presumed Marta and Riccardo had left in the boat, they were surprised when the pair descended unusually late from the roof.

Marta's face, it seemed, had been pressed against the sun. Riccardo's hands were now firm as rock. She announced that they were going out in the boat and, to Derek's observation that it was late, replied "What's it matter, honey?"

"Marta going someplace special tonight?" added Riccardo, half insolent, half carefree.

Derek watched them drop from sight down the steps and went to the parapet when the motor spat. Something kept him there: he practised his golf swing with an imaginary club until they were a splinter driven into the sunset's apricot fuzz. He turned his back to Sandy, who had been trying to interest Sirikit in a trailed skein of wool and, elbows cocked, worked his arms as if pulling pensively on muscle strengtheners. When he removed his glasses and took another swig of the seared wine he had the glazed expression of one who has been looking too long into a blinding light.

Derek stumbled over the explanation of why he had taken so long to raise the alarm. Disappearance of Riccardo's boat in the stage-set sea seemed impossible. He had suspected a romantic escapade but was confident Marta would return, if for no other reason than to receive an award at a Sicilian film festival: a tourist-boosting affair for which many film stars were called and all were chosen. Finally, however, on the third day after their departure, he contacted the police. Soon the coastguard and the press were on the prowl. An illustrated weekly hired a helicopter to take Derek on the search for his vanished wife. There were shots of Derek piloting the machine. A journalist with a scowl like a devil mask, who had checked reports that Marta shot at anyone trespassing on the villa's waterfront, suggested it was a case of better to seek than to find. He assumed it was all a publicity stunt.

It was only after the first frenzied activity had subsided into a routine hopeless search that Derek thought he may have had a magic deliverance. It put his talents to the test to wear the right face for various audiences but the hope that Marta would never return grew apace.

He did not have to pretend with Sandy whom he considered a matter-of-fact young woman. She was restful after Marta, it was like living with a practical, easy-going brother; My Man Friday he told himself. He anticipated he would have to tumble her but merely wanted her around as an assurance of normalcy.

As the threat of Marta's return receded, Derek found himself free to write about her in a way which mixed the excitement of their first months together with the image of her created in the film studios for famished masses from Beirut to Bogota. Every now and again he also provided a glimpse of her impregnable bitchiness.

He gave attention to Sandy's comments with a sincere, brown-eyed willingness to learn which would, as Sandy wrote to her mother, make any girl feel like a million dollars. But what he was learning were the suburban expectations of the torrid affair between Marta and himself. Gradually an avid Marta began to dominate his autobiography.

Now that Marta was becoming identical with her screen image, Derek felt less compulsion to play his classical records and to write sententious much-corrected, retyped letters to acquaintances. He swam a lot with Sandy and took her to bed with him.

Try as she would, Sandy did not find it exciting. Maybe Derek took more care in his younger days. She had the impression that he thought it was expected of him and that he enjoyed more the fathom-deep sleep into which he quickly fell afterwards. His harsh snoring made her long for earplugs as she lay awake wondering whether it had always been a race between him and Marta to sleep first.

But Sandy was not going to let Derek's bed performance spoil their relationship. She carried on as if nothing had happened. If a little old in bed, in other ways Derek was rejuvenated. His drinking dropped, he became affable, he was a man who had begun to believe in his luck again.

Sandy felt encouraged to read him passages from her mother's letters. She had first done so when her mother had written to say she hoped Marta was found and that Sandy was not in danger. They had had a good laugh over that. In the following letter, Mum was scenting out the danger: she wanted to know what Sandy intended to do now.

"Mum says Marta's death reminds her of Harold Holt's and after that things have got steadily worse," Sand read out brightly. The white of Derek's laughing teeth showed up well against his tan. Sandy was sure he would like her mother. She could imagine Derek all of a sudden bussing her flustered and pleased mother as he used to assail his interviewers.

Sandy worried about how to present Dad to Derek and Derek to Dad. For one thing, although he appeared much younger, Derek was nearly Dad's age; for another, Dad was such a wreck. But he might pull himself together for the occasion and not exude an unfocused resentment.

Sandy fed Derek items of news from home judiciously to build the best possible impression of her family and to placate his suspicion. She now felt strong nostalgia even though she came from the western suburbs, out of sight of the sea, where Sydney was no longer Sydney. The longing was augmented by the gums and wattle growing in the villa's garden.

Derek inquired about Sandy's family to see if it resembled the knockabout troupe from which he had escaped. He even enjoyed contemplating a possible life in the lucky country as long as he did not have to actually budge from his Capri patio.

The autobiography now had a sense of direction. It was definitely something an agent could knock into shape. Sandy ensured Derek was fit for the work: they played endless ping-pong and she severely rationed his pasta intake.

Results were not slow in coming: the New York agent cabled on receipt of the Marta episodes that it would go as a book, as a film and maybe as a musical comedy. Derek and Sandy ate out on the strength of that and Sandy hoped he would now pay her salary which had stopped with Marta's disappearance.

After that cable, Derek withdrew a little from their no-nonsense camaraderie but Sandy did not take offence. She admired the new dynamism with which he excised the fatty matter from the earlier sections of the typescript. "I'll serve them the crap *they* want," he told Sandy, "and I'll write just what *I* want next time."

Before either Sandy or Derek expected it, he was summoned to Rome to advise on the casting of the film. Apparently his agent had convinced a producer to rush one out before the memory of Marta disappeared as completely as she had.

Derek was jubilant as he left. Sandy was piqued that he was not taking her along but tried to regard him as a Capri-Rome commuter husband. However she was edgy during his absence: she found the birds, tortoises, rabbits and cats stupid and mournful; she wrote bitsy letters to friends and explained to her mother that she continued to work for Derek because big developments were in store.

The first two days Derek rang to say all was going

well, then there was a dragging silence for three days until a lunch-time call came from Naples. Derek's voice echoed as if in a sea-shell. Excited or drunk, he said he had a friend with him, a friend from the film, "What's his name? " Sandy asked. "Melanie," he answered, then hung up.

All afternoon Sandy sat ostensibly reading a paperback but in fact watching the steps where she would catch her first glimpse of Melanie. She feared she would be a reincarnation of Marta at the beginning of her career. What could be more inevitable than that Derek would fall for the actress chosen to play Marta when she was most provocative?

Sandy tried to convince herself she was being too anxious. More likely Melanie was an assistant director, one of the technical crew, probably a friend of both Marta and Derek, a sensible body in flat heels and sober clothes. There must be some sane people in the film world to keep it spinning, thought Sandy, who had not yet met any.

Melanie could be a scriptwriter, she decided, because, after all, Derek was the author and would have to be consulted on the adaptation. A scriptwriter, she imagined, would be a sharp, serious person with glasses poised on the end of her nose, patient in handling sensitive authors. But if she was so serious why had Derek sounded so strange?

Sandy found no answer to this and other questions as she sat or paced through the hours they made her wait. It took only two hours at the outside from Naples to the villa, she repeated over and again, but Derek and Melanie did not arrive until sunset.

She was disconcerted by the sight of Melanie. The first thing she noticed was her copper hair which shone in the sun and flowed free, straight and strong over her shoulders. At the same time Sandy took in her soaring thighboots of glistening black leather. Sandy considered them ridiculous in the heat but had to admit they created an effect. They finished barely below an earth-brown mini-skirt which for its length and adherence, might have been a singlet. She had big features in a small face dominated by blue, gogglelike sunglasses.

With one arm Melanie held a black strap-bag, with the other, Derek. She moved her bony body with an insolent freedom which threatened Sandy.

Sandy knew she should have gone forward to meet them but she was not equal to it. She stood her ground until Derek, out of breath, introduced Melanie. She gave Sandy a beautifully manicured hand with unpainted fingernails. Sandy noted its reptilian coldness.

The next eighteen hours formed a wild montage in Sandy's mind. Seated in the piazza the following morning, she ran through the scenes again and again to reduce the shock. She had been irritated by Melanie's quick responsiveness to Derek; her familiar habit of squeezing his hand and taking his arm as if physical contact between them was normal; her brazen way of reclining on the couch. When Derek played a classical record, Melanie had danced a shake close to him but abandoned it asking for something less corny. Derek had taken it all like a tantalized rabbit.

Melanie did not speak any language. She used a mixture of Spanish, English, Italian and French, but she got her message across. She had been blankly indifferent to Sandy who wanted to scream at her that she was an Australian like Derek. But it would not have meant much to Melanie who, laughing, described Derek as "mi muy distinguido amigo". Sandy tried to discover something about Melanie's origins but gave up unsure whether Melanie was reluctant or unable to answer. She concluded Melanie was one of those aliens who make themselves at home everywhere.

Finally Derek had made for their bedroom with Melanie. Sandy had shouted then at Derek whose answer was on the level of "Jees, don't be a spoilsport". She had cried tears of rage and self-pity in the room she used to occupy before Marta's disappearance, then fell into a dead sleep from which she awoke only when morning was well advanced.

She had dressed hurriedly, then had gone to the double bedroom to take the revised autobiography and return it to Derek only when he paid her back salary. Still dulled by sleep on entering, she had jolted awake when she found the typescript had been removed, then noticed the accessories strewn around the room: the red wig draped on the wooden bulb of the bed-end, making it look like a shrunken Indian head, and the false eyelashes lying like centipedes in a dish on the dressing table. Sandy was looking at the jackboots beside the bed, which seemed to signify a German officer slept there, when Melanie emerged from the shower recess.

Melanie stark naked was something altogether different: she looked as if she had been shelled for she was smaller and whiter; she had close-cropped black hair; her short eyelashes reminded Sandy of a blowfly; she was boyish. She smiled and so did Sandy who wondered if Derek was now hunting on the other side of the fence. "Sorry," said Sandy whose morale was rising, "I was looking for something but it's not here."

Derek had asked Sandy to stay on, saying there would now be a lot of secretarial work, but when she declined he had, to her surprise, paid most of the back salary.

It had been a swift operation and now Sandy was convalescing in the piazza in the midday sun. Had her mother been right all along? Had she merely imagined it all with Derek? Or should she have stood fast until he tired of jackboots and red wigs? While shouting at Derek had she screamed "Be your age! " just as her mother did when father was in one of his teasing bouncy moods? Or was her memory playing tricks? She was too exhausted to search for the answers but, as she sat letting her coffee cool, she was aware that there was something else to decipher. Half-understood phrases from the previous evening echoed in her head such as "Sister Sandy never shimmied like that" and "just a tryout to see if she can play your part" until they coalesced in the certainty that Melanie was to be Sandy in the film, the with-it secretary of the sexy couple in their Capri retreat. Sandy did not feel up to untying the knot of implications and was depressed at the thought that Derek would always be playing himself. But she knew that in future she needed more substantial nourishment than irony and illusion.

Her daydream was broken by an Italian asking

whether the seat beside her was free and, before she could answer, sitting in it. He had blue drainpipe trousers and matching sports shirt which must have been stitched on. He was blond with blue eyes but Sandy suspected the hair was dyed. As she had seen him occasionally with Riccardo's group, he was probably something between a waiter and a *gigolo*. He asked if she objected to his sitting there. When she gave a non-commital answer which would have discouraged a more sensitive soul, he began holding forth in Italian.

He shut up finally but showed no sign of leaving. Sandy guessed that he wanted to be seen sitting with her. All of a sudden she was curious to know what he thought of Riccardo's disappearance. He asserted that Riccardo would return, as if he had inside information and thought Sandy also was in on the scheme.

He told Sandy that he could recommend a suitable hotel whose owner was a friend. "You have what friends you like there," he said, using English to get through to the rather wooden girl.

"I'm on my way out, thanks," said Sandy. "I've seen more than enough of Capri — it's strictly for the birds."

Perhaps he did not understand. He said with a mixture of pride and resentment: "I slept Michele Morgan."

Sandy laughed, perhaps at the irrelevance or because she was relieved, fearing that this too might have been a fairy story.

"And I slept Derek Nash," she answered as if it was the best joke of all. "I wouldn't recommend it for you."

"What is that? " He had been surprised by her answer.

"Nobody you or anybody else need know," said Sandy but as she spoke she realized that her bitterness was ebbing.

He insisted on buying her another coffee although she had intended to leave immediately. She remembered saying to Derek, while fresh from her disappointment in Naples, that Italians were different. Perhaps they are, she told herself, perhaps they are, thank God. At home he would be in a fruit shop, she thought looking at her companion, but he was quite nice really.

She probed again about Riccardo but decided her companion knew nothing, it was just that he did not want to admit mystery.

Now that she was leaving, she looked about the piazza with new eyes and decided that, given another chance, she could enjoy it in a way she had missed. The tourist season was nearly over and there were no regular boatloads of visitors riding up the funicular, spreading across the square, rushing towards the Faraglioni like lemmings.

The amenity of the salon-like piazza looking beyond the parapet to the distended blue sky got home to Sandy as if she were only now fully present. At least the sky is tender, she reflected, noting that the outlines of buildings were not as sharply etched against it as in Sydney. But all the same it was too much the picture postcard.

Her coffee-buyer had made a gesture towards steering her into bed but she felt it was mainly conventional. He was more than anything companionable, particularly as he had run out of words, and they sat watching the sun edge back the remaining shadow.

If she did not move now, she decided, she would find it more and more difficult. She wanted to avoid the sight of Derek promenading Melanie. Her companion carried her suitcase even though she had made to do so.

"Where are you going? "

She did not know but felt she had been on an island too long and must rejoin the mainland. The idea of a swift return to Sydney was out; she had had a drastic cure for her nostalgia. Rome might be a different story. Her coffee companion shook hands with her at the funicular as if apologizing on behalf of Capri.

She tried to still her panic at the sight of the funicular's cables. She always felt anything continuous like that, an endlessly unwinding chain, as a threat.

By reflex, she felt the nudge of a further anxiety: what if another Derek were on the way? A minor edition of God Almighty in nine months' time! How to introduce a wizened version of Derek to Mum and Dad, especially without Derek making the scene? An undeniably real sequel when she only wanted to zoom off to elsewhere. Derek was just the sort of fool who would blithely make that kind of mistake. It would not happen with either Marta or Melanie but, she reflected ruefully, he must have always thought of her as homely.

She was safely in the funicular at last, attached to the island now only by her fears. As it slid away she glimpsed Maddalena join the queue for the following trip.

Sandy thanked God that Maddalena had not mounted. As always she was dressed in black, as if she were in mourning, and her face expressed the usual unending patience. At the time of Marta's disappearance she had occupied a small corner in some magazines for the quaintness of her comment that she was not surprised by the turn of events.

She must be miserable, thought Sandy, if she feels anything at all, stuck here without an escape route. Sandy, instead, had all Europe ahead of her and who knows how many Dereks in her path.

Maddalena knew, however, that constancy was her strength. It was merely a matter of resisting until she would finally be reunited with Riccardo.

The only return, however, was that of Marta. Every now and again her films were revived, in progressively poorer cinemas, but she remained eternally youthful and radiant. In one of them Riccardo also made a brief, flickering appearance as a cowboy. But Maddalena saw them all for they confirmed her belief that she was dealing with a powerful, alien magic.

More New Fiction

From Australia's leading creative publishing house, UQP

Pieces for a Glass Piano, stories by Gerard Lee
"A most enjoyable book...bawdy, shocking, philosophical, understanding...the author never loses his Rabelasian humour."
John Orrell, *Cairns Post*
"Lee writes with a genuine and effective comic voice."
Australian Book of the Day

Walking through Tigerland, stories by Barry Oakley
Australia's funniest writer in the opinion of critic John Douglas Pringle.
"The style, put to both comic and serious uses, is here so swift and penetrating that it creates a continuity which enables the book to be read like a novel...This is a rare book." David Rowbotham, *Courier-Mail*
(Reprinted within weeks of publication)

Where the Queens All Strayed, a new novel
by Barbara Hanrahan
"One of Australia's most stylish, original and sensitive writers."
John Miles, Adelaide *Advertiser*

The See-through Revolver, a powerful novel by writer and journalist Craig McGregor. One of the top ten fiction bestsellers soon after publication.

Something in the Blood, stories of Australians in Papua New Guinea before Independence by Trevor Shearston. Gritty, often amusing, always readable.

Out Soon

1915, a novel by Roger McDonald – a brilliant and authentically based narrative which shows Gallipoli as it has never been seen before. Compulsive and unforgettable reading.

War Crimes, a long-awaited new collection by master storyteller Peter Carey (author of *The Fat Man in History*)

Among Others Also Available

Johnno, by David Malouf. "An outstanding novel...gloriously readable." David Rowbotham, *Courier-Mail*

The Fat Man in History (4th printing), stories by Peter Carey. "Imagination fired with genius." Robert Adamson, *Australian*

Living Together (3rd printing), by Michael Wilding. "The best of the talent emerging from Down Under." *San Francisco Review of Books* (Other Wilding titles from UQP: *Aspects of the Dying Process* and *The West Midland Underground*)

Flame and Shadow, Selected Stories of David Campbell. "Prose written by a master of words." Brian Elliott, Adelaide *Advertiser*

Contemporary Portraits, stories by Murray Bail. "Brilliantly original." A.R. Chisholm, *Age*

A Place Among People, by Rodney Hall. "The poet writing a novel: the prose is stunning." Mark MacLeod, *Sydney Morning Herald* (Hall's novel *The Ship on the Coin* also from UQP)